High Praise for the Books of LAWRENCE BLOCK!

9-21-18

"No one writes the hard-boiled thriller better than Lawrence Block."
—*The San Diego Union*

"Lawrence Block is a master of crime fiction."
—*Jonathan Kellerman, author of* A Cold Heart

"As good as the crime thriller gets."
—*San Diego Union-Tribune*

"Block writes very well indeed. His dialogue crackles like an overheard conversation in a New York bar."
—*Washington Post Book World*

"Block generates nonstop suspense."
—*Publishers Weekly*

"He is simply the best at what he does… If you haven't read him before, you've wasted a lot of time. Begin now."
—*Mostly Murder*

"No writer conveys the streets, saloons, stationhouses, furnished rooms, deserted churches, and lost sheep of this city better."
—*The New York Daily News*

"Lawrence Block is addictive. Make room on your bookshelf."
—*David Morrell, author of* First Blood

"Remarkable… The suspense is relentless."
—*Philadelphia Inquirer*

"Deliciously amusing."
—*Robert Ludlum*

"Lawrence Block is a master of entertainment."
—*Washington Post Book World*

Grifter's Game

by **Lawrence Block**

ORIGINALLY PUBLISHED AS 'MONA'

A HARD CASE CRIME NOVEL

Mʊ̄ɔ̄

A HARD CASE CRIME BOOK
(HCC-001)
September 2004

Published by

Dorchester Publishing Co., Inc.
200 Madison Avenue
New York, NY 10016

in collaboration with Winterfall LLC

Cover painting copyright © 2004 by Chuck Pyle

ISBN 0-8439-5349-7

The name "Hard Case Crime" and the Hard Case Crime logo
are trademarks of Winterfall LLC. Hard Case Crime Books are
selected and edited by Charles Ardai.

Printed in the United States of America

Visit us on the web at www.HardCaseCrime.com

This is for Loretta

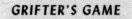

GRIFTER'S GAME

1.

The lobby was air-conditioned and the rug was the kind you sink down into and disappear in without leaving a trace. The bellhops moved silently and instantly and efficiently. The elevators started silently and stopped as silently, and the pretty girls who jockeyed them up and down did not chew gum until they were through working for the day. The ceilings were high and the chandeliers that drooped from them were ornate.

And the manager's voice was pitched very low, his tone apologetic. But this didn't change what he had to say. He wanted the same thing they want in every stinking dive from Hackensack to Hong Kong. He wanted money.

"I don't want to bother you, Mr. Gavilan," he was saying. "But it is the policy of the hotel to request payment once every two weeks. And, since you've been here slightly in excess of three weeks—"

He left that one hanging in the middle of the air, smiling and extending his hands palms-up to show me that he didn't like to talk about money. He liked to receive it, but he didn't like to talk about.

I matched his smile with one of my own. "Wish you'd told me sooner," I said. "Time flies so fast a man can't keep up with it. Look, I want to get upstairs and change now. Suppose you have the bill ready for me when I come back downstairs. I have to go to the bank anyway. Might as well kill two birds with one stone, so to speak. Pick up some money and settle my tab for the moment."

His smile was wider than mine. "Of course, we'll be happy to take your check, Mr. Gavilan. That is—"

"No point to it," I said. "My account's with a Denver bank. It'd take weeks before the check would clear. But I've got a draft on a bank in town. So just have the bill ready when I get downstairs and I'll pay you in cash later this afternoon. Good enough?"

It was definitely good enough. I walked over to the elevator and settled myself in it without calling out my floor. When you stay at the Benjamin Franklin for a day or two, the operator remembers where you live.

I got off at the seventh floor and found my room. The chambermaid hadn't gotten around to it yet and it was the same mess I had left behind me when I went down for breakfast. I sat on the unmade bed for a minute or two, wondering just how much the tab was going to come to at Philadelphia's finest hotel. One hell of a lot, no matter how I figured it. Better than three weeks at ten dollars a day. And better than three weeks of signing for meals, signing for the liquor room service sent up, signing for laundry service and dry cleaning and every other service Philadelphia's leading hotel had to offer. An impressive sum.

Maybe five hundred dollars. Maybe less, maybe more.

One hell of an impressive sum.

I reached into my pocket and found my wallet. I took out my money and counted it. It came to a little over a hundred bucks. And, needless to say, there was no draft on a Philly bank, no account with a Denver bank, no stocks, no bonds, no nothing. There was a hundred bucks plus, and that was all there was in the world.

I found a cigarette and lighted it, thinking how lucky I was that they'd carried me for almost a month without hinting for money. Most people get picked up on less than that. Fortunately, I was cagy and I had been playing it cool. I didn't just come on like a deadbeat. That's important.

For instance, I never signed for tips. Two reasons for that. For one thing, I didn't see any percentage in conning bellhops and waitresses who were probably as broke as I was. And when people sign for tips they get watched closely. Everybody watched them.

So I tipped in cash and I tipped heavy—a buck to a bellhop, a straight twenty percent to a waitress. It was expensive, but it was worth it. It had paid off.

I got out of my clothes and went into the can for a shower. I took the hot spray first, then the cold. I like showers. They make me feel human.

While I toweled off I looked at myself in the mirror. The front was still there—the hard body, the sloping shoulders, the suntan, the narrow waist, the muscle. I looked solid and I looked prosperous. My luggage was top-grain cowhide and my shoes were expensive. So were my suits.

I was going to miss them.

I got dressed in a hurry and I put everything on my back that I could. I wore plaid bathing trunks under my slacks and a knit shirt under the silk one. I stuck cashmere socks—two pairs of them—between my feet and my shoes. I wore my best tie and stuck my second best tie in my pocket. I used all four tie clips on it—the jacket covered them up.

And that did it. Anything else would have made me bulge like a potato sack, and I did not want to bulge. I stuck the wallet in my pocket, left the room a little messier than it had been, and rang for the elevator.

The manager had my tab ready for me when I hit the lobby again. It was a big one. It came to a resounding total of six hundred and seventeen dollars and forty-three cents, a little more than I had figured. I smiled at him and thanked him and left, mulling over the bill as I walked.

The bill, of course, was made out to David Gavilan.

David Gavilan, of course, is not my name.

I needed two things—money to spend and a new town to spend it in. Philly had been kicks, but things just hadn't panned out for me there. I'd spent a week looking for the right angle, another week working it, and the third week finding out that it was a mistake to begin with.

There was a girl in it, naturally. There always is.

Her name was Linda Jamison and she smelled like money. She had short black hair and wild eyes and pretty breasts. Her speech sounded like finishing school. She looked well and dressed well and talked well, and I figured her for Main Line or something damned close to it.

But she wasn't Main Line. She was just sniffing around.

It was a panic, in its own quiet way. I picked her up in a good bar on Sansom Street where the upper crust hobnob. We drank gibsons together and ate dinner together and caught a show together, and we used her car, which was an expensive one.

Things looked fine.

I dated her three days straight before I even kissed her. I was setting this one up slowly, building it right. I am twenty-eight already, too old to be fooling around. If I was going to score I wanted to do it up brown. Maybe even marry her. What the hell—she wasn't bad to look at and she looked as though she might even be fun in the sack. And she smelled like money. I liked money; you can buy nice things with it.

So I kissed her a little on the fourth date, and kissed her a little more on the fifth date, and got her damned bra off on the sixth date and played games with her breasts. They were nice breasts. Firm, sweet, big. I stroked them and fondled them and she seemed to enjoy it as much as I did.

Between the sixth date and the seventh date I used my head for something more than a hatrack. I ran a Dun & Bradstreet on her at a cost of ten whole dollars, and I discovered that the Main Line routine was as queer as a square grape. She was a gold-digger, and the silly little bitch was wasting her time digging me. Clever little moron that I am, I was wasting time and money digging *her*. It would have been funny except that it wasn't.

So the seventh date was the payoff all across the board. I took her out again, and in her car, and I managed to drive around for three hours without spending a penny on her. Then I drove the car to her apartment—a sharp little pad that was evidently her investment in the future, just as the room at the Franklin was mine. We went into her apartment and wound up in the bedroom after not too long.

This time I was not playing games. I got the dress off, and I got the bra off, and I buried my face in bosom-flesh. I got the slip off and I got the garter belt off and I rolled down the stockings. I got the panties off and there was nothing on the bed but little Linda Jamison, the girl of my dreams.

The battle was won, but I was still damned determined to play it to the hilt. I ran a hand over her, starting at the neck and winding up at the Promised Land. She moaned happily, and I don't think that moan was an act. She was hot as a sunburn.

"Linda," I said softly, "I love you. Will you marry me?"

Which made her ecstatic.

From there on in, it was heaven and a half. I came at her like a bull at a matador and wrapped myself up in velvety skin. She made love with the freshness of an impatient virgin and the ingenuity of a sex-scarred whore. Her nails poked holes in my back and her thighs almost choked me.

It took a long time. There was the first time, wild and free, and it was very good. There was in-between, with two heads sharing a pillow and wild sweet talk in whispers. The sour note was the fact that we were both lying like rugs. But it was fun just the same. Don't misunderstand me.

And then there was the second time—controlled now, but still more passionate. If that is possible. It was, underneath it all, a very strange sort of lovemaking. We were playing games, and I knew what the score was and she only knew half of it. It was hysterical.

Maybe it would have been worth it to string her along for a little while. She was good, damned good, in case I haven't managed to make that point yet. I could have gone on dating her, gone on sleeping with her for a week or so. But the game had already been won and the sport was losing its excitement. I decided to get it over with.

We were lying on the bed. I had one hand on her breast. It felt nice.

"Linda," I said, "I . . . I lied to you."

"What do you mean?"

"I know it won't matter to you," I said. "If I didn't know you so well, I probably wouldn't be able to risk telling you. But I do know you, my darling, and there's no room for secrets between us. I have to tell you."

Now she was getting interested.

"Linda," I said, "I am not rich."

She tried not to do a take, God bless her. But I had a

handful of breast and I could feel her stiffen when the words reached her. I almost felt sorry for her.

"I put on an act," I said. "I met you, you see, and I fell for you right off the bat. But there was such a gulf between us. You were rich and I was churchmouse-poor. I didn't figure I had a chance with you. Of course, that was before I knew you. Now I realize that money doesn't matter to you. You love me and I love you and nothing else is the least bit important. Right?"

"Right." She did not sound very convincing.

"But now," I said, "I had to tell you. You see, I had no idea things would progress that fast. I mean, here we are, and we're going to be married. So I had to let you know that I had . . . well, misrepresented myself, so to speak. I know it won't make any difference to you, but I wanted to tell you."

And from that point on it was no contest. When I called her the next day, nobody answered her phone. I went to her building, checked with the landlord. She had moved out, bag and baggage, and she had left no forwarding address. She was two months behind rentwise.

It was hysterical.

So now it wasn't quite as funny as it had been. Now I was on the street myself, close to broke, with no discernible prospects. It was summer and it was hot and I was bored. I needed a change of scene, a new place to operate. It had to be a town close by but out of the state, a town I knew and a town that wouldn't remember me. Too many towns remembered me. The list grew every few months.

Then I had a thought. Atlantic City. Three years ago, a

Mrs. Ida Lister, pushing forty but still shapely, still hungry, still a tiger in the hay. She had reimbursed me quite amply for two weeks' worth of stud services. She had picked up all the tabs, popped for a new wardrobe, and hit me with around five hundred bucks in cash.

The jewels I stole from her set me up for another three thousand bucks.

Atlantic City.

A cruddy little town. A three-way combination of Times Square, Coney Island and Miami Beach. It was hardly the most exciting place in the world.

But it was a dollar or so away from Philly by train and on the right side of the Jersey line. It was a resort town, a town filled with floaters and a properly neutral shade of gray. It was a new place to connect. Properly, this time. No more fooling around. No more winning the battles and losing the war. No more games with chesty chickens like Linda Jamison.

I got in a cab and told him to take me to the railway station. He hurried along on Market Street and I wondered when the flunkies at the Franklin would realize I had skipped.

It was a slow train but it didn't have very far to go. It passed through Haddonfield and Egg Harbor and a few more towns I didn't bother to remember. Then we were pulling into Atlantic City and the passengers were standing up and ready to roll.

The sun was hot as hell and I couldn't see a cloud in the sky. I was glad I'd worn my bathing suit. It would be good to get out of my suit and into the water. I've always liked to swim. And I look good on the beach. It's one of my strong points.

I was out of the railway station before I realized something. I needed to stay at a hotel, and I couldn't stay at a hotel without baggage. Oh, I *could*—but not very well. Without luggage it's strictly a pay-as-you-go proposition, and at the type of place I had in mind the tab was going to come to fifteen dollars a day without meals, twenty with. Rates are high in resort towns in the tourist season. Sure, there are rattraps anywhere, holes where a room is two bucks a day with no questions asked. But that wasn't for me. If you go anywhere, you go first-class. Otherwise there's no point in going, to begin with.

Luggage. I could pick up a second-hand cardboard suitcase in a hockshop, fill it with old clothes and a phone book or two. But that wouldn't do me a hell of a lot of good. The big hotels frown when a guest checks in with cheap luggage. The chambermaids don't go wild over a suitcase filled with phone books.

I had no choice.

I walked back into the railway station, walked in slow. There was a line at the luggage counter and I joined it. I looked over the merchandise set on display and tried to pick the best. It wasn't hard. Two matching suitcases, monogrammed LKB, nestled on the top of the counter. They were top-grade stuff, almost new. I liked the looks of them.

I took a quick look around. Mr. L. K. B. was taking a leak or something; nobody seemed to be interested in his luggage, including the attendant.

I took both bags.

It was that simple. No baggage check, nothing. I picked up the bags, tossed the attendant a buck, and strolled off. Nobody questions a buck tipper. Not an attendant who gets crapped on five times a day for forty bucks a week. The attendant wouldn't even remember what luggage I had taken, and I'd be long gone before L. K. B. realized just what had happened. People take their time putting two and two together, and even so they generally come up with five.

A cab took me to the Shelburne. A doorman opened the door and took my bags. A bellhop took them from the doorman and walked me over to the desk. I gave the desk clerk a quick smile and asked for the best available single. I got it. He asked me how long I'd be staying and I told him I didn't know—a week, two weeks.

He liked that.

My room was on the top floor, a pleasant palace big enough for six full-sized people. The furniture was modern, the carpet thick. I was happy.

I took off my clothes, took another shower to get rid of the train smell. I stretched out on the double bed and thought happy thoughts. I was Leonard K. Blake now. A good name, as good as David Gavilan, as good as my own.

I got up, walked over to the window, stared out. There was the boardwalk, and on the other side of the board-walk there was the beach, and on the beach there were people. Not too many people on this stretch of beach, because it was private—reserved for guests of the Shelburne. No rubbing elbows with the garbage. Not for Leonard K. Blake. He went first-class.

There were men on the beach, and there were girls on the beach, and there were children on the beach. I decided that it was about time there was *me* on the beach. It was too hot a day to sit around the hotel, air conditioning notwithstanding. I needed a swim and I needed some sun. Philly has a way of turning a tan complexion to a sallow pallor.

I put the swim trunks back on, hung up the suit in the closet, put the rest of the stuff I'd brought with me in the dresser drawer. I stuffed L. K. B.'s bags in the closet. I could unpack later and find out what little goodies I had inherited from him. From the looks of the luggage, his clothes would be good enough to wear. I hoped he was my size.

I took the bathers' elevator to the beach level and accepted a towel from another faceless attendant. The Shelburne had a private pathway from the hotel under the Boardwalk to the beach, which was handy. I found a clear spot, spread out my towel, and played run-do-not-walk into the water.

It was a good day for swimming. I let the waves knock me over for a while, then got up the strength to fight back and give them a run for their money. I gave that up, stretched out on my back and floated. I managed to stay awake, though. An uncle of mine once tried floating on his back at Jones Beach and fell asleep. The Coast Guard picked him up fifteen miles off-shore. So I stayed awake.

After awhile, staying awake got to be a bit of a chore. I got out of the water and clambered up on the beach like a walrus with leaden arms. Or forelegs. Whatever it is that walruses have. And I found my towel and stretched out on my stomach.

And fell blissfully asleep.

Her touch woke me. Not her voice, although much later I remember having heard it while I slept, about the same way you can remember the ringing of an alarm clock that you never got up to turn off.

But her hands woke me. Soft hands on the back of my neck. Fingers drumming out not-too-complex rhythms.

I rolled over and opened my eyes.

"You shouldn't sleep like that," she was saying. "Not in this sun. You'll get a bad burn on your back."

I smiled. "Thanks."

"You don't have to thank me. I wanted to wake you up. I was lonely."

I looked at her. I looked at the very good body in the one-piece red suit. The suit was wet and it hugged her like an old friend. I looked at the blonde hair that was blonde all the way to the roots. I looked at the mouth. It was red and wet. It looked ravenously hungry.

And, out of habit, I looked at the fourth finger of her left hand. There was a mark there from a ring, but she wasn't wearing the ring now. I wondered whether she had taken it off before coming to the beach, or when she spotted me.

"Where's the husband?"

"Away," she said, her eyes laughing at me. "Away from me. Not here. I'm lonely."

"He's not in Atlantic City?"

She reached out a finger and chucked me under the chin. She was just a little too good-looking. That bothered me. When a woman's beauty blinds you, your work suffers. A certain part of your anatomy leads you around. That can gum things up.

"He's in Atlantic City," she said. "But he's not *here*."

"Where's here?"

"The beach," she said. "Where *we* are."

Where half a hundred other people also were.

"Want to go swimming?"

She made a face. "I already did," she said. "It's cold. And my bathing cap is too tight. It gives me a headache."

"So go without one."

"I don't like to. I hate to get my hair wet. Especially with the salt water. You have to wash forever to get it out and it ruins the hair. I have very fine hair. I mean the hairs are thin, that is. I'm not complimenting myself."

"You don't have to," I said. "Everybody else must do that for you."

That one got the smile it had to get. A little experience and you learn the language. You have to.

"You're sweet," she said. "Very sweet."

"Isn't your husband sweet?"

"Forget him."

"How can I? He's married to the most beautiful girl in the world."

Another smile.

"Well?"

"He's not sweet. He's old and he's fat and he's ugly. Also stupid. Also revolting."

It was quite a list.

"So why did you marry him?"

"He's also rich," she said. "Very rich. Very very very rich."

We forgot her husband. She did, anyway. I didn't, because he was an important part of the picture. The fat, ugly, old husband, who was also rich. The pretty wife, who wanted more than the old husband was giving her. It was almost standard.

The deviations from the norm were small ones—they only bothered me a little. For one thing, she was too young. Not too young to marry a rich old goat, because you can do that at any age. But too young to chase.

She was twenty-four—or twenty-five or twenty-six or twenty-seven. It was perfectly logical for her to be married to the old goat, perfectly logical for her to be interested in getting into the sack with somebody else.

But at her age, and with her looks, she shouldn't be the one to do the pursuing. She didn't have to be chaste, but she should at least be chased, to coin a phrase.

Later on, when the years went to work on the high breasts and the clear skin, then she could get into the act a little more. She could do the chasing, and she could do the paying. But at this stage of the game there were plenty of guys who would chase her without any encouragement whatsoever, plenty of guys who would bed down with her without expecting to be paid for their labors.

Of course, we hadn't talked about payment yet. We hadn't even talked about bedding down.

We were swimming.

Anyway, we were in the water. Her bathing cap was trying to save her fine blonde hair from the horrors of the salt water; and the two of us were busy letting the waves knock us over. Then, of course, she wanted to learn how to swim, and I wanted to teach her.

I held out my hands and she stretched across them, learning to float on her stomach. She managed to lie with her breasts on one of my arms and her thighs across the other. I could feel the sweet animal warmth of her even in the cold water.

"Like this?"

I told her she had it down pat.

"Now what do I do?"

"Move your arms."

She moved more than her arms. She moved them in an overhand crawl so that her breasts bounced around on my arm. She kicked gently with her long legs and her thighs worked on the other arm.

I wondered who was getting a lesson.

We clowned around some more. She told me her name was Mona and I told her my name was Lennie. She was a lot of fun, besides being a sex symbol. From time to time I even managed to forget that she was somebody else's wife, a potential meal ticket. I thought we were just two nice people having fun on a beach.

Then I would remember who she was and who I was and the pleasant illusion would fade and die.

"Lennie—"

We were on the sand again and I was drying her back with a big striped towel.

"I have to get back to the room, Lennie. I think he's waiting for me. It's been a while."

I knew who *he* was.

"When can I see you again, Mona?"

"Tonight."

"Can you get away?"

"Of course."

"Where and when?"

She thought for all of three seconds. "Right here," she said. "At midnight."

"Isn't the beach closed at night?"

She smiled at me. "You're a clever man," she said. "I'm sure you can find a way to get out here all by yourself. Don't you think so?"

I thought so.

"Midnight," she said. "I hope there's a moon tonight. I like it when there's a moon."

She turned and left. I watched her go—she had a good walk, just a step on the right side of whorishness, as much provocation as a woman could get away with without looking like a slut. I wondered how long it had taken her to learn to walk like that. Or if it was natural.

The sun dried me. I walked back over hot sand to the passageway, through the passageway to the bathers' entrance. I tossed my towel back to the attendant and smiled at him. I rode up in the elevator to the top floor and walked to my room. I had buttoned the room key into the pocket of my swim shorts. I brought it out, wet, and opened the door.

I took another shower, this one to get rid of the salt water. It took longer than it should have, because the hotel had a cute set-up whereby you could take a salt water shower or a fresh water shower, depending upon how you felt about life in general. I goofed the first time around. It was a nice shower, but it left me as salty as ever. Then I figured out the system and rinsed with fresh water.

By the time I was done it was time for dinner. The idea of wearing the same damn clothes I'd worn on the train didn't particularly appeal, and I decided to have a look at L. K. B.'s donation. With luck, his clothes might fit. With more luck, he might have packed some cash in his suitcase. Some people do, believe it or not.

The bags were locked. But suitcase locks, like trunk locks, are all the same. I found a key that fit the little bag and opened it.

Whoever the hell he was, he was the wrong size. His pants were too short and too big in the waist and the behind. His underwear fell off me. But his feet, God bless him, were the right size. There were two pairs of expensive shoes in the little bag and they both fit me. There were also ten pairs of socks which I didn't bother to try on. If the shoes fit, the socks would fit. Unless the guy had very unusual feet.

That took care of the little bag. I put his junk in my drawers and stuck the bag back in the closet. I got the big bag and propped it up on my bed, then opened it with the key.

I hung up the jackets in the closet without looking at them. I was pretty sure they wouldn't fit anyway, and I didn't want to chance running into the bum with his jackets on. Shoes and socks he wouldn't notice, whoever he was. A suit he might.

I got lucky again with his shirts. We were built differently, he and I, but his arms were the same length as mine and his neck the same circumference. His shirts fit me, and he had a lot of shirts. I put them in the drawers.

There was the usual junk—tie pins, cuff links, shirt studs, miscellaneous junk. I went through everything and put everything away. His clothes were from New York and I wondered if he was, too, or if he simply went shopping there.

Then I came to the box.

I thought of money, first of all. It was a small wooden box made of teak or mahogany and it was about the same size and shape as a dollar bill. I took a deep breath and prayed that it held a stack of hundreds. Maybe the bastard was a doctor and he wasn't depositing his receipts, working some kind of a tax dodge. Maybe a hundred different things.

The box gave me trouble. It was locked and none of my keys fit it. I gave up fooling around after awhile and set it on the dresser. It was hinged at the back. I had a little file that went right through those hinges.

I started to open the box. Then I stopped, found a cigarette, and lighted it. I was playing a little game with myself. The box was a present, and I had to try to guess what the present was. Money? Pipe tobacco? Fertilizer?

It could be anything.

I took off the lid. There was a piece of tissue paper on top and I removed that right away.

There was nothing under the paper but white powder.

I was completely destroyed. There is nothing quite so compelling as a sealed box. I had the contents turned into a mental fortune, and now old L. K. B.'s box turned out to be a bust. Powder!

Maybe there was something underneath the powder. I got ready to blow it away, and then all of a sudden some little bell rang deep inside my head and I changed my mind.

I stared at the powder.

It stared back.

I managed to finish my cigarette and butt it in an ashtray thoughtfully provided by the management of the Hotel Shelburne. Then I turned back to the box. I put one finger to my lips and licked it, then dipped it gingerly into the powdery substance.

I licked the finger.

It was absolutely astonishing. I blinked rapidly, several times, and then licked my finger again, dipping it once more into the box.

I licked it another time.

There was no mistaking the taste, not now, not after many years. When you work in a racket, even briefly, you learn what you can about the racket. You learn the product, first of all. No matter how small your connection with the racket or how little time you spend with it, this much you learn. I had played the game for two months, if that, in a very small capacity, but I knew what I had on my dresser.

I had approximately sixty cubic inches of raw heroin.

2.

For a few minutes I just stood there and felt foolish. I'd picked up more than a wardrobe at the railway station. I'd picked up a fortune. How much was the heroin worth? I couldn't even begin to guess. A hundred grand, a quarter of a million, maybe more, maybe less. I had no idea and I didn't even want to think about it.

I couldn't keep it and I couldn't sell it and I couldn't give it back. If L. K. B. ever found me with it he would kill me as sure as men make little green virgins. If the government ever found me with it they would lock me up and drop the key in the middle of the China Sea.

I could throw it away. Did you ever try throwing away a hundred grand, or a quarter of a million?

I put the lid back on the box and tried to figure out what to do with it. I couldn't hide it. People who carry around large quantities of heroin are not amateurs. If they search a room, they find what they are looking for. And if L. K. B. and his buddy boys realized I was their pigeon, no hiding place in the room would keep the heroin away from them. And I had to hold onto the stuff. It could be my trump card, the only thing that would keep me alive if they ever caught on. I could use it to work a deal.

I needed a hiding place for the time being, though. I rejected the standard ones, the cute places where a real pro always looked first. The toilet tank, the bed, the outer window sill. I stuck it on the floor under the dresser and tried to forget about it.

I got dressed in a hurry and left the hotel. The store I was looking for was two long blocks off the Boardwalk on Atlantic Avenue near Tennessee. I went in and bought a good attaché case for twenty dollars and change. It was a nice case—I didn't know you could get them that good so far from Madison Avenue.

I lugged the case back to the hotel, bought a pair of Philly papers at the newsstand in the lobby, then went back to my room. The little box with the hinges filed through was right where I'd left it under the dresser. I took it out, wrapped it up tight in paper so it wouldn't come open, and put it in the attaché case. Then I crumpled up paper and packed it in tight so that nothing would rattle around. I used all of the paper, closed the case and locked it up. I made a mental note to get rid of the key. When the time came, I could always break the thing open. But I didn't want to have the key on my person.

I hefted the case a few times experimentally. It was neither too heavy nor to light. It could have been almost anything.

Then I took it back down to the lobby and hauled it over to the front desk. The room clerk waited obligingly while I picked up my case and put it on the desk between us.

"Wonder if you'd do me a favor," I said. "I've got a commercial presentation here that I'm in the middle of. Not valuable to anybody but me, but there's always the chance that somebody might walk off with it not knowing what was in the case. The company would raise hell if that happened. Could you stick it in the safe for me?"

He could and did. He started to write out a claim check for me but I shook my head.

"I'd only lose it," I told him. "I'm not worried about it. I'll pick it up before I go."

I gave him a dollar and left him with a safeful of heroin.

I had time to kill and thinking to do. I left the hotel again and took a walk on the Boardwalk. If anything, it was worse than when I'd been in town three years back. There were more hotdog and fruit juice stands, more penny arcades, more bingo games and carney booths and flashy souvenir shops. Sex was also present. The professionals stuck to the bars on the side street, but the amateur competition cluttered every board on the Boardwalk. Young girls walking in twos and threes and fours; blondes who got their hair from bottles; fifteen and sixteen and seventeen-year-olds with their blouses too sheer and their blue jeans too tight, their makeup too thick and their strut too obvious. Victory girls who didn't know the war had been over for fifteen years.

The boys were there because the girls were there. They played a game as old as the world, the boys trying to score, the girls trying to be scored upon without looking cheap about it, as though there was a way in the world for them to look otherwise. The boys were clumsy and the girls were clumsier, but somehow they would manage to get together, manage to find a place to neck and pet and make sloppy love. The girls would get pregnant and the boys would get gonorrhea.

One hotel had a terrace facing on the Boardwalk with umbrella-topped tables and tall drinks. I found an empty table and sat under the shade of the umbrella until a waiter found me, took my order, left me and returned with a tall cool vodka collins. It came with a colored straw and I sipped it like a kid sipping a malted. I lighted a cigarette and settled back in my chair. I tried to put everything together and make it add up right.

If I had a tighter connection with a branch of the narcotics trade it would have been easier. A while back I'd done a few jobs for a man named Marcus. It was strictly messenger-boy stuff—pick up this, take it there, give it to so-and-so. I hadn't seen Marcus in years and I didn't know where he was. He probably wouldn't even remember me.

That made selling the stuff impossible.

My other connection was L. K. B. I didn't know who he was, but I had an idea that it wouldn't be too hard to find out. He had arrived just that day, and he had probably checked into a hotel already. All I had to do was run down the list of recent arrivals at the six best hotels in town. Somebody would have those initials, and he would be my boy. I could get in touch with him from a distance, try to work a deal with him and sell his own stuff back to him.

It might work. It also might get me killed. The best I could hope for was a few thousand, a slim fraction of the value of the stuff. And I would spend the rest of my life waiting for a knife in the back.

I didn't like that.

I sipped more of the drink. A man walked by with a girl on his arm. Two old ladies rolled by in a rolling chair pushed by a bored attendant. Victory girls passed, looked at me, decided I was too old, and hurried on with their tails twitching.

I decided to sit tight. For the time being I was in the clear. The way things stood, the worst that could happen was that I skipped the hotel and left them with a box of heroin. If everything broke right, I could get out with a box in tow, hold it for a few years until everybody forgot about it, then find a way to sell it off a little at a time without raising anybody's eyebrows.

In the meantime there was Mona. I thought about her and remembered that she would be on the beach at midnight, waiting for me. I almost forgot the heroin, just thinking about her.

I dropped a buck for the drink and some change for the waiter on the table, and I left. Two blocks further along the Boardwalk I found a good restaurant where they served me a blood-rare steak and very black coffee. I lingered awhile over a second cup of coffee, then went out and found a movie.

The movie was lousy, a historical epic called *A Sound of Distant Drums,* a technicolor cinemascope package with pretty girls and flashing swords and people getting themselves killed flamboyantly. I dozed through most of it. It was a little after ten when I finally got out and headed for the hotel.

I doubled around behind the hotel, found the passageway to the beach and walked through it. There was a pier that ran from the Boardwalk to the ocean and I stayed close to it so that nobody would see me from the Boardwalk and remind me that I wasn't supposed to be on the beach. It was a silly rule to begin with, but Atlantic City was that kind of a town, built with the aid of a stopwatch. The beach closed at a certain hour, the pools in the hotels closed at a certain hour, the world folded up and disappeared at a certain hour. An insomniac could lose his mind in Atlantic City. Even the television shows went off the air at one o'clock.

The beach was empty. I walked down to where the water met the land and watched the waves come in. The sea is hypnotic, like the flames in a fireplace. I don't know how long I stood there, watching the waves without moving a muscle or thinking a thought. I remember that the wind was cold, but that I didn't mind it.

I gave up the game finally, walked back a few steps onto the beach, took off my jacket and made a pillow out of it. I was early—she wasn't due until midnight. If she was coming at all. I wondered about that.

I stretched out on sand and propped up my head on

my jacket. I let my eyes close and let my body relax, but I did not fall asleep. I dozed a little.

I barely heard her coming because my mind was on something else. When I did hear the feet on the sand I knew it had to be her. I lay there without moving and listened to her moving.

"You're always sleeping," she said. "Sleeping all the time. And now you're ruining your clothes. That's not very intelligent of you."

I opened my eyes. She wore a very simple red dress and no shoes at all. The moonlight played on her and showed me how stunning she was.

"We can lie on this. You can ruin your suit all you want, but I'd hate to get this dress all sandy."

For the first time I noticed the blanket she was carrying. I grinned.

"Aren't you even going to get up?"

I stood up and looked at her. She started to say something but stopped with her mouth hanging open. I could understand it. There was something electric in the air, something neither of us could have put into words. Small talk was suddenly impossible. I knew it and she knew it.

I took a step toward her. She held out the blanket and I took hold of two corners and walked backwards. We spread the blanket on the sand and straightened up and looked at each other some more. The electricity was still there.

I wanted to say something but I couldn't. I am certain that it was the same for her. It would have been like talking through a wall. First we had to tear down the wall.

Then there would be a time for talking.

I pulled my shirt out from my pants. I started unbuttoning it. I got it off and let it fall to the sand. I turned to her and she came close, reaching out a hand and touching my chest.

Then she turned around and asked me to unhook her.

I had trouble with the hook-and-eye at the top of the dress. My hands weren't working properly. Finally I managed it. I unzipped the dress all the way down past her waist but I didn't touch her skin at all.

She shrugged and the dress fell from her shoulders.

"The bra, Lennie."

I took off the bra for her. It was black. I remember liking the contrast of the black bra and the pale skin. Then I turned away and took off the rest of my clothes.

When I turned to her once again we were both naked. I looked at her, all of her. I started at the face and looked all the way down past breasts and waist and hips to bare feet. Then I came back up again and my eyes locked with hers.

No words.

We walked toward each other until our bodies touched. I wrapped her up in my arms and held the sweetness of her against me. The silly voices of a thousand people drifted down from the Boardwalk like words from a brainless dream. The waves pounded behind us.

She kissed me.

And then we sank together to the blanket on the beach and forgot the world.

°

I was lying on my side looking over the beach to the sea. Above the water the moon was almost full. Her panties were a wisp of black silk on the sand beside me. I watched the waves and listened to her breathing.

I felt very strange, very weak and very strong at once. I remembered why I had come to Atlantic City in the first place, and I remembered all the things I had done for so many years, and everything seemed foolish, silly. I remembered, incongruously, Mrs. Ida Lister. I had slept with her, too, in Atlantic City. Not on the beach, but in a plush, air-conditioned hotel room. Not because I wanted to, but because she was picking up the tab.

It had all been so stupid. Not wrong, not immoral. Merely stupid. And so had the years of skipping hotel bills, and living on the edge of the law, and looking for the one big connection that would make everything all right.

Now, somehow, the connection had been made. I could see clearly for the first time. Things looked different now.

"Lennie—"

"I know," I said.

"It was—"

"I know, Mona. For me, too."

I rolled over to look at her. Her body was not the same. Before it had been something to desire, something to break down into its component parts of breasts and hips and thighs and belly and behind, something to assess. Now it was *her* body. Now it was a body I had known. It was her.

"I can't stay much longer."

"Why not?"

"Keith. He'll wonder where I am. He won't care, but he'll wonder." Her voice was very bitter.

"Is that his name? Keith?"

She nodded.

"How long have you been married?"

"Almost two years. I'm twenty-five. We were married two years ago this September. I was twenty-three then."

She said it as though she was thinking that she would never be twenty-three again.

"Why did you marry him?"

Her smile was not a happy one. "Money," she said. "And boredom, and because twenty-three isn't eighteen any more, and all the other reasons. Why do pretty girls marry rich old men? You know the answer as well as I do."

I found a pack of cigarettes in my jacket pocket. They were crumpled. I took one out and straightened it out, then offered it to her. She shook her head. I lighted it and smoked for a moment or so in silence.

"Now you go back to him?"

"I have to."

"And then what?"

"I don't know."

"Then we meet here every midnight for a week or two," I said. "And each night you go back to him. And then the two of you go away and you forget me."

She didn't say anything.

"Is that how it goes?"

"I don't know."

I dragged on the cigarette. It didn't taste right and I buried it in the sand.

"This hasn't happened before, Lennie."

"This?"

"Us."

"So we let it go?"

"I don't know, Lennie. I don't know anything any more. I used to know all the answers. Now somebody changed the questions."

I knew what she meant.

Her voice was very distant now. "We have a house in Cheshire Point," she said. "On a two-acre lot with big old trees and expensive furniture. My clothes cost money. I have a sable coat and an ermine coat and a chinchilla stole. We didn't even bother with mink. That's the kind of money Keith has."

"How did he make it?"

She shrugged. "He's a businessman. An office downtown on Chambers Street. I don't even know what he does. He goes downtown a few times a week. He never talks about the business, never gets mail at the house or brings work home. He says he buys things and he sells them. That's all he says."

"What do the two of you do for kicks?"

"I don't know."

"You have a lot of friends? Congenial companionship? Bridge parties on Saturday nights and steaks in the back yard?"

"Stop it, Lennie."

"Are you going back to Cheshire Point with him? To

share his bed and have his kids and spend his money? Are you—"

"Stop it!"

I stopped it. I wanted to reach for her, to roll her up in my arms and tell her that everything was going to be all right. But I didn't believe it myself.

"I'll have one of those cigarettes now, Lennie."

I took out two, straightened them out, gave her one and kept one for myself. I scratched a match for her and cupped it in my hands. She came over to accept the light and I looked down at the top of her head and thought how beautiful she was. I envied Keith and realized that he would envy me. It always works that way.

"It probably doesn't mean anything anyway," she said. She was talking to herself now, not to me. "It was just once. It happened, we were both ready for it, it was good. But it didn't mean anything. I can forget you and you can forget me. In a week we would forget each other. It doesn't mean a thing."

"Do you really believe that?"

Silence for a moment.

Then, bitterly, "No, of course not. No, I don't believe it."

"Would you leave him?"

She smiled. "I'd leave him in a minute," she said. "But that isn't what you mean. You mean will I leave his money."

I didn't say anything.

"Do you have any money, Lennie?"

"Fifty dollars. A hundred, maybe."

She laughed. "He spends that much on a whore."

"What does he need one for? He's got you for a wife."

I didn't realize how that sounded until I heard it. I watched her face fall. "I suppose you're right," she said. "He doesn't need a whore. He's married to one."

"I didn't mean that. I—"

"But it's true." She took a deep breath, then let it out. She stuck her cigarette in the sand and straightened up. "I can't leave him, Lennie. I've got all that money and I can't let go of it. It wouldn't work."

I didn't say anything.

"Two years," she said. "Why didn't I meet you two years ago? Why?"

"Would it have made a difference?"

"A big difference," she said. "Money is funny. That rhymes, doesn't it? But it's true. I wasn't born this way, Lennie. I could have lived without money. People manage. If I had met you before I met Keith—"

"If this blanket had wings we could fly it."

"Or if it was a magic carpet," she said. "But don't you see what I mean? Now I'm used to money. I know what it's like to have it. I know what it's like to be able to do anything I want and buy anything I want. I couldn't go back to the way it was before."

"How was it before?"

"It wasn't that bad," she said. "I wasn't deprived. We didn't starve. We owned our own home, never worried about eating regularly. But we didn't have money left over. You know what I mean."

I knew what she meant. And I wondered what I was

doing, trying to convince her to throw it up and marry me. So we could starve hand in hand? So we could raise children and live in a frame house in Yahooville? So I could carry a lunch pail to work and owe the bank and the finance company and everybody else in the world? For what? For a girl who didn't even know my real name?

But I heard myself say, "It could work. We could make it work, Mona."

She looked at me, her eyes very bright. She was about to say something that never got said. I wondered what it was.

Instead she got to her feet and began to put clothes on. I watched her while she dressed.

"I'll leave the blanket here," she said. "The hotel won't miss it. It would look funny if I came in carrying a blanket." She was looking at me now. "I have to go," she said. "I really have to go."

"Do I get to see you again?"

"Do you want to?"

I wanted to.

"I'll . . . I'll get in touch with you. Somehow. But I have to go back now."

"To Keith."

"To Keith," she echoed. "To being his wife. To being Mrs. L. Keith Brassard."

I barely heard her. I watched her go, watched that perfect, half-whore, half-lady walk of hers carry her up the beach alongside the pier. I watched her and thought about her and thought about myself, and I wondered what had happened to the two of us, and what was going to happen from here on in.

She was almost to the Boardwalk before I remembered her final words and realized hysterically just who her husband was.

L. Keith Brassard.

3.

I folded the blanket very methodically until it was a little cushion two feet square. I planted my rump on it and sat at the edge of the shore looking out on the water. I wanted to run out into the water and swim like a maniac until I wound up in some place that was not Atlantic City.

He's a businessman. An office downtown on Chambers Street. I don't even know what he does.

She would be back by now, taking the elevator up to her room. I wondered where her room was. Maybe it was on the same floor as mine.

He goes downtown a few times a week. He never talks about the business, never gets mail at the house or brings work home. He says he buys things and he sells them. That's all he says.

I wondered whether or not he had told her about the missing suitcases. It was pretty obvious she didn't know anything about the heroin. If his suitcases were stolen, that wouldn't mean a thing to her. A man who bought her a sable coat, an ermine coat and a chinchilla stole undoubtedly could replace the contents of two suitcases without taxing his budget. A man who lived in Cheshire Point luxury could afford to buy himself a few more suits and a new batch of underwear.

I thought about him and I thought about her and I thought about me. We were each pretty special. L. Keith Brassard—an import-export man with a new slant on life, a tall man in narcotics with a pretty wife and a perfect front. Mona Brassard—a dryness in the throat and a moistness in the palm of the hand, a sweetness that caught at you and strangled you. She wanted me and she wanted money and I don't know how in hell she could have us both.

And Joe Marlin. That was my name, before it was David Gavilan, before it was Leonard K. Blake, before a lot of names. Do names matter? They never did.

But for some damned reason I wanted her to call me Joe.

We were cuties, Dave and Lennie and I. We had the white powder and we had the warm woman. We were riding free and loose. We had everything but a future.

I smoked a cigarette all the way down and threw the butt in the ocean. Then I stuffed the hotel's blanket under the pier and walked back to the Boardwalk.

I picked up the phone in my room and asked room service for a bottle of Jack Daniels and a pail of ice and a glass. I sat down in a chair then and waited for something to happen. The air conditioning was turned all the way up and the room was well on its way to becoming a refrigerator.

There was a knock at the door. The bellhop was there, a wiry kid with quick eyes. He put the bottle of bourbon and the bucket of ice on the dresser, then gave me the tab. I signed for it and handed him a dollar.

Except for the eyes he was a college boy on summer vacation. The eyes knew too much.

"Thanks," he said. Then, "Anything you want, I can get it for you. The name is Ralph."

He left and I settled down with the Jack Daniels.

I put a pair of ice cubes in a water tumbler and poured three ounces of bourbon over them. While the ice cooled the liquor I sat back in a chair and thought about things. Then I started my drink. The liquor was smooth as silk. The label on the bottle said they filtered it through charcoal or something. Whatever they did to it, it worked.

I drank some more and smoked a little. The liquor loosened me up until my mind started working again, fishing around for answers, finding new questions to ask.

I should pack up, get out, forget her. But I knew that if I left, I would never find her or anyone like her again. Before, I had managed to live without her. But now I had had her. How had she put it?

Don't you see what I mean? Now I'm used to money. I know what it's like to have it. I know what it's like to be able to do anything I want and to buy anything I want. I couldn't go back to the way it was before.

I had had her—once—and I was used to her. I knew what it was like to have her, to love her and be loved by her. Love? A weird and shifty word. It made me feel like the hero of a popular song.

But I couldn't go back to the way it was before.

She was right and I was right; only the world was wrong. We needed each other and we needed that money, and if there was a way to get both I didn't know where to find it. I tried looking for it at the bottom of the glass but it wasn't there. I filled the glass again, skipping the ice this time around. The liquor was smooth enough without it.

I had the heroin. I could take it to New York and sniff around in the wrong streets until I made a connection, then unload for all I could get. It might work. The money might be enough, enough to take us away from L. Keith Brassard. Enough to get out of the country—South America, or Spain, or the Italian Riviera. We could live a long time on the money. We could buy a boat and live on it. Once, I learned how to sail. There is nothing like it. And you can take a boat and lose yourself in a million little islands all over the world, islands where it's always warm and the air is clear and clean. We could go anywhere.

And we could never look behind us.

Because we would never get away. He was not an ordinary husband, not a straight Westchester burgher with a lawful mind and lawful friends. Anybody carrying that much horse was very well connected indeed. The word would go far and wide, and there would be an unofficial but firm price on a certain man and a certain woman. Some day somebody somewhere would look twice at us. We could run but we could not hide.

We wouldn't last long that way. We'd start off loving

each other very hard, and then every day we would do a little more private thinking about the men who were going to catch us. It wouldn't happen all at once—we'd forget those men, and then something would happen that would force the memory of them upon us, and we would run again.

And then it would begin to happen. She would remember being Mrs. L. Keith Brassard and living in Cheshire Point with her ermine coat and her sable coat and her chinchilla wrap, with a big solid house and heavy furniture and charge accounts. She would remember how it felt not to be afraid, and she would realize that she had never been afraid before she met me; that she was always afraid now, a little bit more afraid with every passing day. Then she would begin to hate me.

And I would remember an uncomplicated life, where you left one town when things became overly difficult, where the biggest threat was a watchful hotel manager, and the biggest problem the next meal. I would look at the soft sweetness of her and I would think about death—a slow and unpleasant death, because the men he would send would be experts at that sort of thing. And, inevitably, I would begin to hate her.

I couldn't have her and I couldn't have the money, not that way. I drank more bourbon and thought about it and drew blanks. There had to be a way, but there wasn't.

The bottle was half-gone when I thought of the way, the only way. Another person might have thought of it at once, but my mind has certain established channels in which it runs and this was out of known waters. So it took a bottle of Jack Daniels before I got around to it.

Brassard could die.

That scared the hell out of me, and I had two more quick drinks, got out of my clothes and into bed. I fell asleep almost at once. Maybe the liquor was responsible for that. I don't know. Maybe I slept because I was afraid to stay awake.

I was dreaming, but it was one of those dreams you forget the minute you come awake. The knocking at the door woke me up and the dream slipped away from me. I opened my eye very tentatively. I wasn't hungover and I felt fine. At least I would have, given a few hours more sleep.

The knocking began again.

"Who is it?"

"Chambermaid."

"Go away." Great hotel, when the chambermaids wake you up in the middle of the morning. "Come back next year."

"Open the door, Mr. Blake—"

"Go play in traffic. I'm tired."

The voice changed to a coo. "Lennie," it said, "*please* open the door."

For a minute I thought the dream was back again. Then I jumped out of bed and wrapped up in a sheet. She looked cool and fresh in a white cotton blouse and a pair of sea-green clam-diggers. She came right on in and I closed the door.

"You're nuts," I said. "For coming here. But of course you know that."

"I know."

"He could have seen you. He'll wonder where you went. It wasn't too brilliant of you."

She was smiling. "You look silly," she said. "Wrapped up in that sheet like an Arabian sheik. Were you sleeping?"

"Of course. It's the middle of the night."

"Middle of the day, you mean."

"What time is it?"

"Almost noon," she said. "And he couldn't have seen me, anyway. He was out of the hotel at the crack of dawn. Business, he said, something unexpected. Even in Atlantic City he has business. Business before pleasure. Always."

I knew what business he had. A whole boxful of business that had neatly disappeared.

She pouted. "Aren't you glad to see me?"

"You know the answer to that one."

"You don't *seem* glad. You didn't even kiss me hello."

I kissed her. And then it all came back, all the way back, and it was the night on the beach all over again. One kiss did that. She was that kind of woman.

"That's better."

"Much better."

Very deliberately she removed the blouse and the clam-diggers, kicked her shoes under my bed. She wasn't wearing anything else. I couldn't stop looking at her.

Her eyes were laughing. "You silly man," she said. "You don't need that silly sheet, do you?"

I didn't.

o

Much later I opened my eyes. She was curled up like a sleeping kitten with her blonde hair all disorganized on the pillow. I reached out a hand and ran it over her body from shoulder to hip. She didn't stir.

I reached over for the pack of cigarettes on the table at the side of the bed. I found a match and lighted a cigarette. When I turned back to her she had her eyes open.

She smiled for an answer.

"You're pretty great, you know."

Her smile widened.

"I'm going to miss you."

She bit her lip. "Lennie—"

I waited.

"Remember what I told you on the beach? That I couldn't give up the money?"

I remembered.

"I found out something today. Here. With you."

I waited some more.

"I . . . still can't give up the money."

The cigarette didn't taste right. I took another drag and coughed on it.

"But I can't give you up either, Lennie. I . . . don't know where we go from here. I want the money and I want you and I can't have both. I'm a spoiled little girl. I can't *do* anything. All I can do is want."

I knew what the answer was and I knew that I was scared to hand it to her. But the die was cast. I couldn't see the spots, couldn't tell whether we had come up with seven or whether we had crapped out royally. Either way, the pattern was there already. It couldn't be changed from here on in.

"How old is Keith?"

She shrugged. "Fifty," she said. "Fifty-five. I don't know. I never asked him. That's silly, isn't it? Not knowing how old you own husband is. Fifty or fifty-five or something around there. I don't know. Why?"

"I was just thinking."

She looked at me.

"I mean . . . he's not a young man, Mona. Men his age don't live forever."

I left it like that, hanging in the middle of the air, and I watched her face try not to change expression. She didn't quite make it. It was terrifying, in a way. We were a little too much alike. We had both been thinking of the same thing. I guess it had to be that way.

"Maybe his heart isn't too good," I went on, talking around the whole thing. "Maybe some day he'll fall on his face and it'll be all over. It happens every day, you know. It could happen to him."

She fed my own words back to me. "If this bed had wings we could fly it, Lennie. Or if it were a magic carpet. His heart's in perfect shape. He goes to the doctor for a physical three times a year. Maybe he's afraid of dying. I don't know. Three times a year he goes to the doctor, spends the whole day there getting the most complete physical examination money can buy. He went less than a month ago. He's in perfect physical shape. He was bragging to me about it."

"He could still get a coronary. Even when you're

in perfect shape—"

"Lennie."

I stopped and looked at her.

"You don't mean he could have a heart attack. You mean something else."

I didn't say anything.

"You mean he could have an accident. That's what you mean, isn't it?"

I drew on the cigarette. I looked hard at her and tried to figure out a way to fit all the pieces together. If there was a way to do it, I couldn't find it. The pieces had jagged edges and they didn't mesh at all.

"I wish we weren't us," she was saying now. "I wish we were other people. Other people wouldn't think rotten things. This is rotten."

I left it alone.

"I don't love him, Lennie. Maybe I love you. I don't know. All I know is I want to be with you and I don't want to be with him. But he's . . . a good man, Lennie. He's good to me. He isn't mean or cruel or vicious or—"

He was a dope peddler on a grand scale, an import-export cookie who imported the wrong thing. He was a top link in a cutie-pie game that sent high-school kids out doing armed robbery to pacify the monkey he put on their shoulders, a game that had caused more human agony than all other cutie-pie games combined.

But she didn't know this, and I didn't know how to tell her about it. And therefore he was a good man, not mean or cruel or vicious.

"What do you want to do now?"

What she wanted to do was change the subject. She had a good way to do it. She put out her arms for me and forced a smile.

"We've got a few more hours," she said. "Let's spend them in bed."

It seemed like a pretty good idea at the time. But after awhile I dropped off to sleep and she didn't. I shouldn't have done that, I guess. It was a mistake. But I wasn't in any condition to do too much deep thinking at the time, and that was a shame.

Because when I did wake up she was shaking me by one shoulder and looking at me all wide-eyed and frightened. I didn't catch on to it right away. I had to hear it before it soaked in.

"Lennie—"

I sat up on the edge of the bed and took her hand off my shoulder. Her nails had been digging into me. I don't think she realized it at the time.

"The bags—"

I don't think too cleverly when I wake up. I was still lost.

"Lennie, what are you doing with Keith's bags in your closet?"

It was a hell of a good question.

She was so confused she couldn't think straight. She stood there bubbling and babbling. I had to slap her twice across the face to calm her down. I didn't hit her very hard, but each time I slapped her it hurt me. Finally I got her to sit down in a chair and keep her ears open and her mouth shut.

There were a lot of things I didn't want to tell her just yet and a few more I'd have preferred never to tell her. But I didn't have any choice. She had seen the L. K. B. bags in the closet. God alone knew what had prompted her to rummage through my closet, but this was beside the point. The point, simply enough, was that the cat was halfway out of the bag and it couldn't hurt to bring it out the rest of the way.

"Don't interrupt me at all," I told her. "This is a long story. It won't make sense to you until you've heard all of it."

I started with getting off the train from Philly and needing luggage. It went back farther than that, went years back, but the rest of it wasn't important. Not for the time being, anyway. If things broke right I would have a whole lifetime to tell her the story of my life. If they didn't, then nothing much mattered.

I told her that I took his luggage at random, checked into the hotel under a phony name, met her, opened his bags, and found the heroin. She didn't believe that part of it at first but I went over it again and again until it made sense. There was a hysterical expression on her face when the news soaked in. She was seeing old Keith in a new light now. He was a dope peddler, not a nice guy. She had managed to live with him for two years without tumbling to this juicy little fact, and she couldn't have been more surprised if I had told her he was a woman.

I ran it from alpha to omega and then I stopped

because there was no more to tell. Her hubby was a crook and I had his supply in the hotel safe. We were together in my room and the world was taking us for a joy ride.

"This changes things, Lennie. Joe, I mean. I guess I have to call you Joe now, don't I?"

"I guess so."

"Joe Marlin instead of Lennie Blake. All right. I like it better. But this changes things, Joe. Doesn't it?"

"How?"

"Now I don't want his money," she said. "I couldn't stand living with him any more. Now all I want is you. We can forget him and just run away and be together forever."

It sounded good but it didn't work that way. She wasn't seeing the whole picture yet. He was still old Keith. Now he made his money in a dirty business and it sickened her. But she didn't see that the man himself was different.

"We'd be killed, Mona."

She stared at me.

"We'd run and we'd be caught. He's a gangster, Mona. You know what a gangster is?"

Her eyes went very wide.

"You're his woman," I went on. "He bought you and he's been paying heavily for you. Ermine coat, sable coat, chinchilla stole. Those things run into money."

"But—"

"So now he owns you. You can't run away. He'll catch you and he'll have you killed. Do you want us to die, Mona?"

I saw the look in her eyes and I remembered the slight contempt in her voice when she talked about Brassard's physical exams. She had said that maybe he was afraid of death. He wasn't the only one. She was afraid of dying herself. That made two of us.

"We can't run," I said. "We wouldn't get away."

"It's a big world."

"The mob is a big mob. Bigger than the world. Where do you want to run?"

She didn't have an answer.

"Well?"

She bit her lower lip. "The accident," she said. "Before you said he could have an accident. Didn't you?"

"I worded it a little differently."

"But that's what you meant. I suppose he could still have an accident, couldn't he?"

"I thought you didn't want to think about things like that."

"It's different now, Joe. I didn't know what kind of a man he was. Now it's different."

It wasn't the least bit different. Before he was kind and generous and now he was mean and vicious. This was the wrapper. It was a game to make murder a little bit easier to swallow. Sugar on a pill. But the pill was the same no matter how goddamned sweet it tasted. The pill was still murder.

"Joe?"

I was starting to sweat. Atlantic City was getting too warm for us and the air conditioning in the room could never change that. I cupped her chin in my hand and tilted her head up so that she was looking at me.

"When are you and Keith going back to Cheshire Point?"

"Joe, I don't want to go with him. I can't go with him, Joe. I have to stay with you."

"When are you going back to Cheshire Point? Just answer the questions, dammit."

"A week. Six days, I don't know."

I played mental arithmetic. "Okay," I said. "First off, you don't see me any more. If we pass on the Boardwalk you don't even look at me. No matter where Keith is, understand? Because he has friends here. I don't want any connection between the two of us. Nobody can see us together or the game is over."

"I don't understand. Joe—"

"If you kept your mouth shut you might have a better chance of understanding."

Her eyes were hurt. But she shut up.

"I'm leaving here the day after tomorrow," I said. "I'm checking out bag and baggage and I'm going to New York. I'll find a place to stay under another name."

"What name?"

"I don't know yet. It doesn't matter. You won't have to get in touch with me. I'll get in touch with you. Just stay put. As far as you're concerned, nothing has happened. Keith is good old Keith and you never met me. Got that?"

She nodded solemnly.

"Don't forget. You have to keep saying it over and over to yourself so that you don't slip out of character. You're Keith's wife. I never happened to you. You're going to go back with him and you're going to be the same woman he took with him to Atlantic City. The same all across the board. You don't know a thing. You got that? You understand the part you're going to have to play?"

"I understand."

Now came the harder part. Hard to tell her, hard to think about. "You'll have to sleep with him," I said. "I . . . wish you didn't. I don't like it."

"Neither do I."

"Maybe you can tell him you're sick," I said. "It might work. But just remember that if this breaks for us you'll never have to sleep with him or look at him or think about him again for the rest of your life. That might make it a little easier."

She nodded.

I hesitated, then looked around for the pack of cigarettes. She wanted one too, which was understandable. I gave her one and took one for myself and lighted them both. We smoked for a few minutes in relative silence.

"Mona," I said, "I'll need money."

"Money?"

"To pay the hotel bill," I said. "I can't afford a skip-tracer on my tail. And I have to get the package of heroin back from the desk."

"How much will it cost?"

"I don't know. And I'll need money to operate on in New York. Not much, but as much as I can get. I hate to ask you for it—"

"Don't be silly."

I grinned. "How much can you spare?"

She thought for a moment. "I have a few hundred in cash. I can let you have it."

"How will you explain it?"

"If he asks I'll tell him I saw some jewelry and wanted it. I don't think he'll ask. He's not that way. He doesn't care what I spend or how I spend it. If I told him I lost it at the track he wouldn't mind."

"You're sure it's safe?"

"Positive."

"Put as much as you can spare in an envelope," I said. "One of the hotel's envelopes. Don't write anything on it. Sometime this evening pass my room. The door will be closed, but not locked. Open it, drop the envelope inside, then beat it. Don't stop to say anything to me."

She smiled. "It sounds like a spy movie. Cloak and dagger. Bob Mitchum in a trenchcoat."

"It's safer that way."

"I'll do it. After dinner?"

"Whenever you get a chance. I'll be here until I get the envelope. I'll leave for New York the day after tomorrow. I don't want to rush things. Good enough?"

"I guess so."

"Get dressed," I said. "I'll see you in New York."

We both got dressed in a hurry. Then I motioned her back, walked to the door and opened it. A chambermaid was strolling down the hall, taking her time. I waited until the maid got out of the way.

Before I sent Mona out I grabbed her and kissed her very quickly. It was a strange kiss—passionless, and surprisingly intense at the same time. Then she was out in the hall heading for the elevator and I was closing the door and walking back toward the bed.

There was a drink or two or three in the bottle of Jack Daniels. I finished off the bourbon and felt a little better.

4.

I got the money a few minutes after six. It was a very strange feeling—I was lying on the bed with the light out, riding along on the slight edge the bourbon had been able to give me. The air conditioner was whirring gently in the background. Then the door opened less than six inches, an envelope flopped to the floor, and the door closed.

I hadn't even seen her hand. And this made the entire affair so impersonal it was startling. The door had opened by itself, the envelope had come from nowhere, and the door had closed. There were no living creatures involved in the process.

I picked up the envelope, shook the contents down to one end and ripped open the other end. Tens and twenties and fifties. I counted them twice and got a total of $370 each time.

They went in my wallet and the envelope went in the wastebasket.

It hit me all at once and I fell on the bed trying not to laugh. It was funny, and at the same time it was anything but funny, and I muffled my face with a pillow and howled like a hyena.

If it was anyone but Mona, it would be so simple. I would smile a happy smile, walk out of the hotel, and catch a train for Nowheresville with three hundred and seventy hard-earned dollars in my kick. When you looked at it that way it was the simplest and deftest con I had ever pulled in my life. Sweet and easy, without a problem in the world.

Except that I wasn't pulling a con. Now, with the money handed to me on a solid gold platter, I was going to pay my hotel bill, play my cards properly, and wind up going to New York and waiting for her. I don't know whether it is funny or not, but I was laughing my fool head off.

When I ran out of laughs I grabbed a shower and shave and went to the hotel next door for dinner. Nobody goes to the hotel next door for dinner. You either eat in your own hotel or you go to a restaurant. That was what I was bargaining on. I didn't want to run into Mona and I didn't want to run into Keith. Not until I was ready for them.

The dinner was probably good. Big hotels cook dependably if not imaginatively. They don't ruin steaks, which was what I ordered. But I didn't taste my dinner. I thought about him and I thought about her and I tasted murder instead of meat. I kept a cigarette going throughout the meal and paid more attention to it than to my steak. I sat staring into my coffee for a long time. Then when I started to drink it, it was room-temperature and horrible. I left it there and went to a movie.

The movie made about as much sense to me as if the actors had been speaking Persian and the sub-titles were done in Chinese. I remember nothing about the story, not even the title. The show was there to kill time and that is all it did. I looked at the screen but I didn't see it. I thought. I planned. I schemed. Call it what you want.

I would have liked to get out of Atlantic City then and there. Staying around was a risk that grew greater every minute that I spent in the miserable town. And, now that I had decided to pay for my room, every extra day was an expense that I couldn't quite afford. Mona's contribution to my welfare, combined with the little money of my own that was left, gave me a drop over four hundred dollars. It was going too fast to suit me.

But I couldn't leave yet. I needed a look at my man, my L. Keith Brassard. I needed to know the enemy before I would decide how and when and where to kill him.

The movie ended and I went back to the hotel. The Boardwalk was a little less heavily populated then usual but as raucous as ever. I stood for a moment or two watching a pitchman explain how you could live an extra ten years if you squashed vegetables in a patented liquifier and drank the crap you wound up with. I watched him put a cabbage through the machine. It started out as a head of cabbage. Then the machine went to work on it. The pitchman flipped the pulpy remains into a garbage pail and proudly lifted a glass of noxious-looking pap to his lips. He drained it in a swallow and smiled broadly.

I wondered if you could do the same thing to a human being. Put him in a patented liquifier and squeeze the juice out of him. Flip the pulp in a garbage pail. Close the lid tight.

I walked on and drank a glass of pina colada at a fruit juice stand. I wondered how they made it and got a frightening mental picture of a pineapple and a coconut waltzing hand in hand into a patented liquifier in a sort of vegetarian suicide pact. I finished the pina colada and headed for the hotel.

A man walked out as I walked in. I caught only the quickest of looks at him but there was something familiar about him. I had seen him before, somewhere. I had no idea where or when, or who he might be.

He was short and dark and thin. He had all his hair and it was combed neatly and worn fairly long. His black moustache was neatly trimmed. He dressed well and he walked quickly.

For some reason I hoped to God he hadn't recognized me.

I saw him the next day.

I woke up around ten, got dressed in slacks and an open shirt and went down to the coffee shop for breakfast. I was starving, strangely enough, and I wolfed down waffles and sausages and two cups of black coffee in no time at all. Then I lit the morning's first cigarette and went out to wait for him.

I went to the hotel terrace where I'd had a drink the

first night. I found a table under an umbrella. It was close enough to the Boardwalk to give me a good view and far enough away so that nobody would notice me unless they worked at it. The waiter came over and I ordered black coffee. It was a little too early for drinking, although the rest of the customers didn't seem to think so. A garment-district type and a broken-down brunette were knocking off daiquiris and whooping it up. Getting an early start, I thought. Or still going from the night before. I forgot all about them and watched the Boardwalk.

And almost missed them.

After your first day in Atlantic City you stop watching the rolling chairs that plod back and forth along the Boardwalk. They're part of the scenery, and it is out of the question that anybody you know might ride in one of them. I had forgotten the chairs, concentrating on the people who were walking, and I barely saw them. Then I got an eyeful of yellow hair and took a second look, and there they were.

He was short and he was fat and he was old. He was also every inch the good burgher from Westchester, and it was no longer hard to see how he had fooled Mona. Some honest men look like crooks; some crooks look like honest men. He was one of the second kind.

He had a firm, honest chin and a thin-lipped, honest mouth. His eyes were water-blue—I could see that even from where I was sitting. His hair was white. Not gray but white. There is something very regal about white hair.

I watched that nice-looking honest old man until the

chair stopped in front of the Shelburne and they got out of it. Then I drank my coffee and wondered how we were going to kill him.

"More coffee, sir?"

I looked up at the waiter. I didn't feel like moving and I didn't feel like more coffee.

"Not just yet."

"Certainly, sir. Would you care for something to eat, perhaps? I have a menu."

When they want you to defecate or abandon the toilet they make no bones about it. I didn't want food and I didn't want coffee. Therefore I should pay the man and go away. They had fifty empty tables on that terrace and they wanted fifty-one.

"Martini," I said, tired. "Extra dry, twist of lemon."

He bowed and vanished. He re-appeared shortly thereafter with martini in tow. There were two olives instead of one and he had remembered the twist of lemon, which most of them don't. Maybe he wanted to be friends.

I don't know why I ordered the drink. Ordinarily I would have left about then. I didn't want a drink, didn't want a meal, didn't want more coffee, and I had already seen Brassard. These factors, combined with my thorough lack of love for both terrace and waiter, should have sent me on my way.

They didn't. And I got another look—a longer and closer one—at L. Keith Brassard.

I don't know how he got there. I looked up and there he was, three tables down, with a waiter at his elbow. My waiter. He was giving me the profile and he looked as solidly respectable as ever.

I sat there feeling obvious as all hell and wished I had a newspaper to hide behind. I didn't want to look at the man. There's an old trick—you stare hard and long at somebody and they fidget for a minute or two, then turn and look at you. It's not extrasensory perception or anything like that. They catch a glimpse of you out of the corner of an eye, something like that.

I was positive that if I stared at him he would turn around and look at me. I didn't want that to happen. Whatever way we played it in New York, I was coming on with one great advantage. I knew him and he didn't know me. It was a trump card and I hated like hell to lose it in Atlantic City.

So I nursed the drink and watched him part-time. The more I watched him the harder he looked at me. You have to be very hard inside if you can get away with looking soft. It's much easier to be a success as a gangster if you look like a gangster. The closer you are to the Hollywood stereotype, the quicker acceptance comes to you. If you look more like Wall Street than Mulberry Street, Mulberry Street doesn't want to see you. He was going to be a hard man to kill. I was chewing the first olive when he got company. There had to be a reason more pronounced than thirst for him to be biding his time on the terrace, and the reason appeared in short order. The reason was short and thin, well-dressed with long hair neatly combed and black moustache properly trimmed. The reason was the man I had half-recognized the night before walking out of the Shelburne. Now I remembered him.

And almost choked on the olive.

His name was Reggie Cole. He worked for a man named Max Treger, and so did half of New Jersey. Treger was a wise old man who occupied a secure and nebulous position at the top of everything that happened in the state of New Jersey on the uncouth side of the law. Treger I knew solely by reputation. Reggie Cole I had met once, years ago, at a party. Reggie was smaller then, but the years and Max Treger had been kind to him. Reggie had risen—he sat at the right hand of God, according to rumor.

Now he sat at the right hand of L. Keith Brassard. I got him full-face that way and I was worried. It had been a long time since that brief meeting, but I recognized him. There was all the reason in the world for him to remember me. I had taken a girl away from him. The girl was a pig and I'm sure he hadn't cared much at the time, but it wasn't something he would forget.

I waited for him to look up and see me. But he and Brassard were busy—they were talking quickly and earnestly and I wished I could hear what they were saying. It wasn't hard to guess the topic of conversation. Brassard was supposed to be delivering enough heroin to keep all of New Jersey stoned for a long time. The horse had miraculously disappeared. Which was sure as hell something to talk about.

I swallowed the second olive whole. I put enough money on the table to cover the martini and the coffee and the waiter, tucking the bill under the empty glass so that it wouldn't blow away.

Just as I was starting to get up, a head came up and small eyes looked at me. A short, puzzled look—probably exactly the same as the one I had given him the night before. A look of vague and distant recognition. He remembered me but he didn't know who I was.

The next time around he would know. I hoped the conversation with Brassard was serious enough to take his mind off me.

I got up and tried not to run. I walked away with my back to the two of them and hoped to God they weren't looking at it. The sweat had my shirt plastered to my back by the time I reached the Shelburne. And it wasn't even a particularly warm day.

There was no point in staying around any longer. I had already gotten more than I'd bargained for—a look at him and a hint of who his buddies were. As well as I could figure it, Brassard had come running to Atlantic City with a cargo of heroin. He wasn't a delivery boy—it was *his* heroin, bought and paid for and ready for resale. Nobody was going to accuse him of welching or anything of the sort. His only headaches were financial ones.

If anything, Max Treger was the man who looked bad. From Brassard's point of view, the only man who could have picked him so neatly was the man who knew what he was carrying. Treger had a solid reputation for honesty-among-thieves and all that, but with that big a bundle hanging fire Brassard was undoubtedly suspicious. I hoped he would raise enough hell so that somebody would get mad and shoot holes in his head. It would save me a lot of work.

But I didn't think it would happen. In a few days Brassard would convince Treger that he wasn't playing heroin hopscotch and Treger in turn would convince Brassard that he had better rackets under his thumb than petty larceny. The two clowns would put their crooked heads together and come up with an unknown quantity. They would start looking for this unknown quantity, at which time it would be very unhealthy to be me.

I wanted to run but it was too early. The big headache was the goddamned luggage. The bags were ordinary enough but they could be recognized especially when the Red Alert went out on them. I didn't give a damn if somebody remembered them in a week or so—by that time I'd be snug in New York with my trail as well-covered as it was ever going to be. But I didn't want anybody to tip until I was as far as possible from Atlantic City.

I gave the railway station a buzz from my room and found out that there was a train to Philly every morning at 7:30. There was another every afternoon, but the morning train was a hell of a lot safer. Everybody is properly asleep at that hour, and at the same time there's nothing suspicious about checking out then, as there would be for a train leaving at, say, four in the morning. The less people who saw my bags on the way out, the better I would feel about it. The less chance of Brassard being around, the happier I was.

I called the desk in the middle of the afternoon to

leave a call for six the following morning, which must have puzzled the hell out of them. Then I phoned room service for more Jack Daniels and let the afternoon and evening spend themselves in a mildly alcoholic fog. It was gentle drinking. I had nothing better to do, and at the same time I had no overwhelming compulsion to get stoned to the earlobes. I paced myself properly and kept a comfortable edge on until I felt tired enough to sleep. Then I threw down a few extra shots and slipped over the edge so that sleep would come a little more quickly. Which it did.

My eyes opened the second the phone rang and I came thoroughly awake at once. I took a salt water shower, this time on purpose, and then chased away the salt with cold fresh water. I used up three little towels before I managed to get dry.

I dressed and went downstairs. There was a different monkey behind the desk but he was just as obliging as the first. He gave me no trouble at all. He handed over the attaché case and I gave him my nicest smile in return.

All the way back through the lobby to the elevator and up too many flights to my room I felt as though half the English-speaking world was staring at the attaché case.

I actually tried to open it, then remembered locking it and consigning the key to limbo. It was a shame. I couldn't very well leave either of Brassard's bags lying around. If the case were open I could transfer the heroin to one of his bags and let the case lose itself. This way I had three bags to carry. It would be no problem at first, but it might be trouble when I switched trains.

I packed all of my stuff and all of Brassard's stuff into his two suitcases. Since I had come with next to nothing, this wasn't the hardest thing in the world. Then I went back down to the lobby, let a bellboy carry my bags to the inevitable waiting taxi, and wandered over to the desk.

The monkey hoped I had enjoyed my stay.

"Wonderful town," I told him, lying in my teeth. "I needed the rest. Feel like a new man."

That much was true.

"Going back home now?"

"Back to Philly," I told him. I'd used a good address off Rittenhouse Square when I checked in.

"Come back and see us."

I nodded. He should sit on a hot stove until I came back. He should hold his breath.

I went out the side entrance. The cab was there with my bags nestled together in the trunk. I gave the bellhop a buck and hoped he would forget all about the luggage.

At the railway station I bought a ticket straight through to Philadelphia. I carried my baggage on the train. It was tough to lug three pieces without looking awkward but I managed it somehow. The conductor came by, took my train ticket and gave me a seat check good to Philadelphia. I settled back and let the train chug its way past Egg Harbor and Haddonfield. Then we were in North Philly and I was leaving the train. Me and my three little suitcases. I remembered the story of Benjamin Franklin as a young man running through the streets of Philadelphia with a loaf of bread under each arm and another one in his mouth. I knew precisely what he looked like. And I hoped Philly was used to the sight by now.

I tried to get excited but I couldn't raise the necessary enthusiasm. There was no problem, no sweat, no headache. Who was going to remember another proper young man with three suitcases? Who would Brassard's men question—commuters? Conductors?

No problem.

If some cutie-pie figured out the orthographic relationship between L. Keith Brassard and Leonard K. Blake, he might trace me through to the railway station, might find a clerk who knew I'd bought a ticket to Philly. But nobody in the world was going to figure that I'd gone to New York.

No problem.

In less than three minutes I was off the train, down the stairwell, through the tunnel, and on the opposite platform. I waited there for less than five minutes before a train for New York pulled up and I got on. I put my suitcases up on the luggage rack and relaxed in my seat. When the conductor came by I let him sell me a ticket straight through to Boston. It wasn't necessary, not in the least, but I wanted to play everything to the hilt.

It sounds like a spy movie. Cloak and dagger. Bob Mitchum in a trenchcoat.

I thought about Mona and wondered how long it would be before I saw her again. I thought about the first time on the beach, and the times in my hotel room. I thought about the way she moved and the tricks her eyes played.

She was right as rain with the Bob Mitchum line. I was overplaying things. We had nothing at all to worry about. I was on my way to New York without leaving a trace of a trail. Brassard was out looking for wrong trees to bark up. We had it aced.

All we had to do now was get away with murder.

5.

I checked into the Collingwood Hotel as Howard Shaw. The Collingwood was a good second-class hotel on Thirty-fifth Street just west of Fifth. My room was thirty-two dollars a week; it was clean and comfortable. I had a central location without being in the middle of things, the way I would have been in a Times Square hotel. I stood that much less chance of running into old familiar faces.

The door clicked shut behind me and I dropped my three suitcases on the floor. I shoved the attaché case under the bed and decided to hope for the best.

The Collingwood was a residential hotel and there were no bellboys to scoop up your bags. Nobody saw the L. K. B. monogram on the luggage on the way up, which was fine with me. Getting rid of the luggage was the next step, of course. It might have been simpler to check them in a subway locker and throw the key away, but they were too good and I was too broke. I ripped the labels out of all of Brassard's clothing except for what fit me, stuffed the clothes into the suitcases, and went downtown to where Third Avenue turns into the Bowery.

I sold better than three hundred dollars' worth of clothing to a round-shouldered, beetle-eyed man for thirty dollars. I pawned two suitcases worth over a hundred bucks for twenty-five. I left Brassard's stuff to be bought by bottle babies, and I went back to my hotel and slept.

It was Thursday. Sunday or Monday they would be coming back to New York. Now they were together at the Shelburne. Probably in bed.

I dreamed about them and woke up sweating.

Friday I looked him up in the phone book. There was a single entry, not even in bold-faced type. It said *Brassard, L. K.* 117 Chmbrs . . . . . . WOrth 4-6363. I left the hotel and found a pay phone in a drugstore around the corner. I dialed WOrth 4-6363 and let it ring eight times without getting an answer. I walked over to Sixth and caught the D train to Chambers, then wandered around until I found 117.

It was the right building for him. The bricks had been red once; now they were colorless. All the windows needed washing. The names of the tenants were painted on the windows—*Comet Enterprises, Inc.* . . . *Cut-Rate Auto Insurance*. . . *Passport Fotos While-U-Wait* . . . *Zenith Employment*. . . *Kallett Confidential Investigations*. . . *Rafael Messero, Mexican Attorney, Divorce Information*. Nine stories of cubbyholes, nine stories of very free enterprise. I wondered why he didn't have a better office. I wondered if he ever came to the one he had.

His name was on the directory. The elevator was self-service and I rode it to the fifth floor. I got out and walked past the employment agency to the door marked L. K. Brassard. The window glass was frosted and I couldn't see a thing.

I tried the door and wasn't particularly surprised to find out that it was locked. The lock was the standard spring lock that catches automatically when you close the door, and there was a good eighth of an inch between the door and the jamb. I looked around at Zenith Employment. Their door was closed. I wondered what the penalty was for breaking and entering.

The blade of my penknife took the lock in less than twenty seconds. It's a simple operation—you fit the knife blade in between the door and the jamb and pry the locking mechanism back. Good doors have the jamb recessed so that this cannot be done. This one was a bad door. I opened it about an inch and looked around again. Then I shoved it open, walked in and locked it behind me.

The office looked like what it was supposed to be. One of the oldest remaining roll-top desks in America stood in one corner. There was an inkstand on it. I looked around hysterically for a quill pen and was almost surprised not to find one.

There were half a dozen large ledgers on the desk and I went over them fairly carefully. I don't know what I expected to find. Whether the entries were coded or merely blinds I couldn't tell. It was a waste of time studying them.

The drawers and pigeonholes of the desk yielded a lot more of nothing in particular. There were bills and canceled checks and bank statements. Evidently he had a certain amount of legitimate business in addition to the main event. From what I could make out, he imported a lot of Japanese garbage—cigarette lighters, toys, junk jewelry, that sort of stuff. That fit into the picture. It was easy to see heroin coming through Japan by way of China or Hong Kong or Macao.

I sat in his leather chair in front of his desk and tried to put myself in his place. What hit me the hardest was the very double life he was leading. He was not a crook in the same sense as, say, Reggie Cole or Max Treger. Everybody who knew Treger knew just what sort of a man he was. He managed to stay out of jail because nobody managed to collect the evidence that would put him where he belonged. But if Treger had a wife, Mrs. T. knew just how her husband kept mink on her back. Some of Treger's neighbors snubbed him while others pretended he was just one of the boys—but they all knew he was a gangster. The people in Cheshire Point didn't know that about good old L. Keith Brassard.

I tapped out a drum solo on the top of that very respectable desk and wondered why the hell I had come to his office in the first place. I didn't know what I'd expected to find, or hoped to find. I wasn't a federal narcotics agent trying to crack a dope ring. I was a wise guy who wanted to kill Brassard and wind up with his wife. So what was I doing there?

I wiped off everything I remembered touching. It probably would never matter, but I didn't want to leave my prints in his office in case they ever tied me to him. There was one scrap of paper I'd found with four phone numbers on it and nothing to tell what the numbers were. I copied them down.

He could tell the office had been entered. I did what I could, but I knew there would be some items out of place. I hoped there was a maid with a key—then he might not suspect a search.

On the way back to the hotel I picked up a few pairs of slacks and some underwear. I found a suit and an extra sport jacket and arranged to have them delivered to me at the Collingwood by Monday. All together the clothes came to over a hundred, and left me with not much money. It hurt to spend that much on clothes, but I couldn't see any way to avoid it. I needed the clothes. And they couldn't be too cheap or it wouldn't look right. Then I picked up a fairly respectable looking suitcase for twenty-five bucks. That hurt too.

By the time I got back to the hotel I felt pretty rotten. I was tired and bored and perspiring. The shower took care of the perspiration but the boredom remained. I had nothing to do and no place to go and I did not like myself very much. And I missed her so much I could taste it.

I had a good dinner with a drink before and a brandy after. Then I went out and bought a bottle and took it to bed.

*

Saturday came and went without my accomplishing very much. I went to a barber and got a crew cut, something I hadn't done in one hell of a long time. When I got back to my room I gave myself a long look in the bathroom mirror. The haircut had changed me more than anything else could have. It made my face rounder, my forehead higher, my whole appearance a good two years younger.

I went down to the drugstore, picked up a handful of paperback novels, went back to the hotel and spent the rest of the day reading, and sipping what remained in the bottle. I had time to kill and I wanted to get it out of the way as quickly as possible. If I could have spent two days in a coma I would have been glad of it. I didn't want to think and I didn't want to plan and I didn't want to do much of anything. I just waited for the time to go by.

Sunday afternoon I walked over to Penn Station and looked her up in the Westchester phonebook. She lived on something called Roscommon Drive. I memorized the number and left.

I called her that evening.

It was a warm night and the fan in the phone booth did not work. I put in a dime and dialed her number and got an operator who sent back my dine and told me to deposit twenty cents. I dropped in the original dime and another one and the phone rang. A man's voice said hello to me.

"Is Jerry there?"

"I'm afraid you have the wrong number."

"Isn't this Jerry Hillman's residence?"

"No," he said. "I'm sorry."

He hung up on me and I sat there in the hot booth hearing his voice again in my mind. It was a cultured voice. He spaced his words and talked pleasantly.

I left the booth and walked around the block. They were home. I took out a cigarette and smoked it in a hurry. I had to get in touch with her and I wasn't sure how to do it. I wondered if his phone was tapped. Most likely it was. I figured he probably tapped it himself. It wouldn't be the first time.

I called again from the same booth and this time she answered it. When she said hello I saw her in my mind and felt her in my arms. I started to shake.

"Is Jerry Hillman there?"

"No," she said. "You must have the wrong number."

She recognized my voice. I could tell.

"Isn't this AL 5-2504?"

"No," she said.

I sat in the phone booth for over fifteen minutes. I held the phone to my ear with one hand to make it look good while I held the hook down with the other. Then the phone rang and I lifted the hook and said hello.

"Joe," she said. "Hello, Joe."

"How has it been?"

"All right," she said. "I suppose. I missed you, Joe."

"I've been going crazy waiting for you. I was afraid you wouldn't catch the number. Where are you calling from?"

"A drugstore," she said. "I . . . I was ready for your call. Keith answered the first time and said it was a wrong number. But I knew it was you."

I took a breath. "I have to see you," I said. "Can you get into Manhattan tomorrow?"

"I think so. He's going to the office. I'll ride in with him and tell him I have to do some shopping. I can get in sometime between nine and ten. Is that all right?"

"Perfect."

"Where are you staying?"

"A hotel," I said. "The Collingwood. Just east of Herald Square."

"Should I meet you there?"

I thought about it for a minute. "Better not," I said. "There's an Automat on Thirty-fourth between Sixth and Seventh. Meet me there."

"Thirty-fourth between Sixth and Seventh. I'll be there. I love you, Joe."

I told her I loved her. I told her how much I wanted her.

"I have to get off now," she said. "I came down to the drugstore to buy Tampax. He'll wonder what's taking me so long."

"Tampax?"

I must have sounded disappointed because she giggled at me with a very sexy giggle. "Don't worry," she said. "It was two birds with one stone, Joe. It was an excuse to go to the drugstore and an excuse to keep Keith away from me tonight. I don't want him touching me tonight, Joe. Not when you're this close to me. I couldn't stand it."

She hung up and I stood there with a receiver in my hand. I walked out of there and tried not to shake visibly.

I stopped at a little bar on the way home and tossed down a double shot of bourbon, then sipped the beer chaser very slowly.

The bartender was a big man with a wide forehead. He was listening to hillbilly music on a portable radio that blared away on top of the back bar. The song was something about a real grade-A bitch who was causing the singer untold heartache. The bartender polished glasses in time to the not-very-subtle rhythms of the song. Two or three guys were doing solo drinking. A man and a woman were drinking and playing footsie in a back booth.

How long since I'd seen her? Less than a week. Five or six days. But you can forget a lot in that amount of time. I remembered what she looked like and what she sounded like and how it felt to hold onto her. But I had forgotten, in part, just how much I needed her.

The sound of her voice had brought all of it back to me. Brought it back forcibly.

I wondered how I would kill him. I would have to be the killer, of course. And I would have to do it alone. She'd be the prime suspect, the first one the cops would get to, and I'd have to make sure she had a perfect alibi.

I could kill him at home or at his office. At home might be better—Manhattan homicide cops are too damned thorough. Westchester homicide would be a little less likely to know what was doing.

How? A gun or a knife? The proverbial blunt instrument? Or would I wring his neck with my hands? I tried to remember whether or not you could get fingerprints on a human being's neck. I didn't think you could.

I started to shake some more. Then I had another double bourbon and another beer and went back to the hotel.

6.

I got to the Automat at nine. The girl in the cashier's cage dealt me a stack of nickels and I wandered around playing New York's favorite slot machines. I filled a tray with a glass of orange juice, a dangerous-looking bowl of oatmeal, a pair of crullers and a cup of black coffee. Then I found a table that gave me a good view of the entrance and started in on my breakfast.

I was working on a second cup of coffee when she showed. I looked at her and my head started spinning. She was wearing a very simple blue-gray summer dress that buttoned up the front. She looked sweet and virginal and lovely, and I waited for her to rush over to my table and wrap herself around my neck.

But she was so cool it almost scared me. She looked right at me and the shadow of a smile crossed her face. Then she swept on past me, broke a quarter into nickels and invested the nickels in coffee and a glazed doughnut. Then she stood with the tray in her hands, looking around for a place to sit. Finally she walked over to my table, unloaded the tray and sat down.

"This is fun," she said. "The cloak and dagger stuff, I mean. I'm getting a little carried away with it."

I had too much to say and there was no convenient place to begin. I started a cigarette to go with the coffee and plunged in somewhere in the middle. "Have any trouble getting here?"

"None at all. I rode in with Keith on the train. I told him I had to do some shopping. Remind me to do some shopping later. I'll buy a pair of shoes or something. Anything."

"It must be nice to have money."

I just threw the line out; maybe it was a mistake. She turned her eyes on me and her eyes said a great many things that cannot be translated too easily into English. Sure, it was nice to have money. It was nice to be in love, too. Many things were nice.

"Joe—"

"What?"

"I was thinking that maybe we don't have to kill him."

"Not so loud!"

"No one's paying any attention to me. Look, there's another way that I've been thinking about. We won't have to kill him if it works out."

"Getting soft?"

"Not soft," she said.

"What then?"

"Maybe scared. I understand they electrocute murderers in New York. I . . . don't want to be electrocuted."

"You have to be convicted first."

Her eyes flared. "You sound as though you hate him," she said. "You sound as though killing is more important than getting away with it."

"And you sound as though you're trying to back out. Maybe that's what you want. Maybe we should forget the whole thing. You go your way and I'll go mine. Buy yourself all the shoes you want. And a few more furs. And—"

And a man sat down at our table. An old man, broken by time, with a frayed collar on his clean white shirt, with spots on a wide polka-dot tie. He very solemnly poured milk over a bowlful of corn flakes and sprinkled two tablespoons of sugar on top of the mess while we watched him with our mouths open.

"Let's go," I said. "Come on."

No matter where you are in Manhattan there is a bar around the corner. There was a bar around the corner now and we went to it. We found the most remote of the three empty booths and filled it. I hadn't wanted a drink; now I needed one. I had bourbon and water and she had a screwdriver.

"Well?"

"You've got everything wrong," she said. "I'm not trying to get out of anything. You can be pretty saintly about this, can't you? You don't have to live with him. You don't—"

"Get to the point."

She took a sip of her drink and followed it with a deep breath. "The heroin," she said. "Do you still have it?"

I nodded.

"We can use it," she said.

"Sell it and run?" I got ready to tell her all over again why that wouldn't work. But she didn't give me a chance.

"Plant it," she said. "Put it in his car or around the house or something. Then you or I would call the police anonymously and tip them off. They would search and find the heroin and arrest him."

A bell rang somewhere but I ignored it. "Just like that?" I said. "Plant it, tip the fuzz, and send hubby off to jail?"

"Why not?"

"Because it wouldn't work."

She looked at me.

"Let's see just what would happen, Mona. The police would run the tip down and find the heroin. Then they'd ask him how it got there, and he'd say he didn't have the vaguest idea. Right?"

She nodded.

"So they'd take him in and book him," I went on. "The charge would be possession with intent to sell. In ten minutes a very expensive lawyer would have him out on bail. Ten months later his case would come up. He'd plead not guilty. His lawyer would tell the court that here was a man with no criminal record, no illicit connections, a respectable businessman who had been framed by person or persons unknown. They would find him not guilty."

"But the dope would be right there!"

"So what?" I took a sip of the bourbon. "The jury would acquit him forty-nine chances out of fifty. The fiftieth—and that's a hell of a long shot—they'd find him guilty and his lawyer would file an appeal. And he'd win on the appeal unless an even longer long shot came in. Even if both long shots broke right—and I'm damned if I ever want to buck odds like that—it would still be two to three years before he saw the inside of a jail for more than five consecutive hours. That's a long time to wait, honey. And there's a damn good chance that sometime during those two or three years he would figure out who tipped the cops. At which time he would find a very capable gunman who would shoot a large hole in your pretty head."

She shuddered.

"So we have to kill him."

"I didn't want to." Her voice was very small.

"You know another way?"

"I thought—But you're right. There isn't any other way. We have to . . . kill him."

I drank to that. I ordered another round and the bartender brought the drinks, bourbon and water for me, another screwdriver for her. I paid for them.

"How?"

I didn't answer her.

"How will we—"

"Hang on," I said. "I'm trying to think." I put my elbow on the table and rested my forehead in the palm of my hand. I closed my eyes and tried like hell to think straight. It wasn't particularly easy. Brassard and money and Mona and heroin were chasing one another around a beanpole with my face. There had to be a way to fit all the pieces together and come out with a plan. But I couldn't find it.

"Well?"

I lighted a cigarette, then studied her face through a cloud of smoke. I rested the cigarette in a small glass ashtray and took her hands in mine. All of a sudden whatever plan I might have thought of became quite unimportant. It was like the first time. And the second time, and every time. I guess *electric* is the right word for it. It was exactly that effect.

Electric. One time I saw a man pick up a lamp cord that had frayed right through to the bare wire. The current glued him and the cord together. He couldn't let go. The voltage was a little too low to kill him, but he remained stuck to that wire until some young genius cut the power.

That's how it was.

"Joe—"

"Let's get out of here."

"Where are we going?"

"My hotel."

"Is that safe?"

I stared at her.

"Someone might see us," she said. "It would mean taking a chance. And we can't afford to take chances."

She knew how much I needed her. And now she was teasing, playing games. I looked at her and watched her turn into a sex symbol in front of my eyes. She did not look sweet and virginal and lovely any more. I looked at the very simple summer dress and saw breasts and belly and hips. I looked at her eyes and saw lust as naked as my own.

"I'll go shopping now," she said. "I'll buy a pair of shoes so that Keith won't wonder why I came to the city. Meanwhile you go back to the hotel and think up a jim-dandy plan. Then you call me and tell me all about it and we'll see what we can work out. That's the safe way."

"To hell with the safe way."

"But we can't afford to take chances. We've got to do it the safe way, Joe. *You* know that."

They were just words and she didn't mean them at all. I stood up without letting go of her hand, crossed over to her side of the booth and sat down next to her. Our eyes locked.

"Joe—"

I put my hand on the very soft skin of her throat. I ran it down slowly over her breasts to her thighs. I pressed her.

"Now," I said. "Now tell me about the safe way."

We caught a cab right outside the bar. It was less than three blocks to the Collingwood but we were in too much of a hurry to walk.

It was almost too good.

Maybe the tension was responsible for it, the tremendous mutual need for something that would push the fear away and postpone the immediacy of what we were planning to do. Maybe some grain of morality imbedded within us both made our adultery as amazingly gratifying as it was.

Whatever it was, I was all in favor of it.

I lighted cigarettes for both of us and gave one of them to her. We lay side by side and smoked them all the way down without saying a word. I finished mine first and stubbed it. It took her a few seconds more. Then she flipped the butt out the open window.

"Maybe I'll set fire to New York," she said. "Maybe the whole city will burn."

"Maybe."

"Or maybe it landed on somebody's head."

"I doubt it. The window opens out on an airshaft. Nobody walks around down there."

"That's good," she said. "I wouldn't want to set anybody on fire."

"Not even me?"

"That's different."

I kissed her face and her throat. She stretched out on her back with her eyes closed and purred like a fat cat in front of a hot fire. I stroked her and she purred some more.

"How, Joe?"

And we were back where we started from. Back to murder. Now, for some reason, it was easier to talk about it. Maybe our lovemaking was responsible for that; maybe strong proof of our mutual need was a means of justifying our actions.

"Joe?"

"Let's talk about Keith," I said. "Has he been acting any different lately?"

"Like how?"

"Because the heroin is missing."

"Oh," she said. "At first he seemed worried about something. He still acts a little . . . well, irritated, I guess."

"That figures."

She nodded slowly. "But he's not doing anything different," she said. Not running around or anything. He's his usual self."

"That figures too. He's not an errand boy. He's an executive. All he can do is pass the word and see what happens."

"I guess so." She yawned and stretched. "So life goes on. He gets up in the morning and reads the paper. Then he does the crossword puzzle. Did I ever tell you about that? He's sort of a crossword puzzle nut. I can't even talk to him when he's working on one of them. Every morning the *Times* comes and every morning it's the same ritual. First the financial page and then the crossword puzzle. And if he's stuck on the puzzle it doesn't matter. He doesn't throw the damned thing out like a sensible person would. He keeps plowing away at it until it's done. He even uses a dictionary. Did you ever hear of doing crossword puzzles with a dictionary? That's the way he does them."

I pictured him at the breakfast table, pencil in hand, dictionary at his side. I could see him working very steadily, filling in all the blank squares with neat letters. Of course he would use his dictionary, and of course he wouldn't quit until he was finished. It was all in character.

"Then he goes to the office," she went on. "Monday,

Wednesday, and Friday. He goes to the office."

I looked up. "I thought he didn't have a regular schedule?"

"He doesn't, exactly. Sometimes he works on a Tuesday or Thursday, if he's busy. But almost every Monday and Wednesday and Friday, off he goes to the office. Then he comes home, and we eat, and it's another dull evening with Mr. and Mrs. L. Keith Brassard. Then it's morning, and another dull day."

She grinned. She reached out a hand and touched me, a gentle touch. I reached for her.

"Not now, Joe. You were going to tell me the plan. How you're going to kill him."

How *you're* going to kill him. Not *we're* going to kill him. But at the time I hardly heard the difference.

"I'm not going to tell you, Mona."

"No?"

I shook my head.

"Don't you trust me?"

I had to laugh. "Trust you? If I didn't trust you there would be no point in the whole thing. Of course I trust you."

"Then tell me."

"I can't."

"Why not?"

Part of the reason was that I didn't know myself. But I didn't want to toss that one at her. There was another reason, and I decided it would have to do for the time being. "The police are going to question you," I told her. "Up and down and back and forth. You're money and class, respectable as all hell, so they won't use the bright lights and the rubber hoses. Not the class-conscious Westchester police. But at the same time he's a rich old man and you're a pretty wife, so they'll suspect you."

"I'll have an alibi."

"No kidding." I went looking for another cigarette and set fire to the end of it. "Of course you'll have an alibi. That's what the cops will figure in the first place. They'll read it for a standard wife's-boyfriend-slays-rich-hubby gambit. Page three in the *Daily News* four days out of five. They'll be quiet, and they'll be polite as Emily Post's little boy, but they will be sharp. The more questions you can say *I don't know* to, the better off we'll both be. The less you know, the easier it'll be to give that answer. So I'm telling you as little as possible."

She didn't say anything. She wasn't looking at me now. She was staring across the room, looking at the far wall. At least it looked that way, but I got the feeling that she didn't see that wall at all. I got the feeling that she was looking right through it, way out into space.

I wondered what she saw.

"Joe," she said.

I waited.

"I'm worried," she said. "I tried not to think about it before. But you're right. Page three in the *Daily News* four days out of five. They'll question me."

"Of course they will."

"Maybe I'll crack."

"Don't be silly."

"Maybe—"

I looked at her. She was trembling. It wasn't a good old-fashioned case of the shakes, but I could see it. I took her in my arms and rubbed the back of her neck. I held her close and stroked her until I could feel the tension drain out of her, and then I kissed her once and let her go.

"Don't worry, Mona."

"I'm all right now. I just—"

"I know. But don't worry. They won't work you that hard. You won't know anything, remember? You'll tell them the same things you told me the first time you met me. You don't know exactly what Keith does for a living. He doesn't have any enemies that you know about. You don't know why anybody would want to kill him. It doesn't make any sense to you. He was your husband and you loved him. Don't overwork the grief bit, but let yourself react naturally. You'll probably be a little sorry once it's done, you know. The normal human reaction. Let it show, but don't milk it."

She nodded.

"Keep calm," I said. "That's the important thing."

"When?"

I looked at her.

"When are you going to do it?"

"I don't know."

"You don't know or you're not telling me?"

I shrugged. "A little of both. Probably this week, probably on one of the days when he goes to work."

"At his office?"

"Maybe. Maybe not. Don't leave the house until he's

off to work. Understand?"

She nodded.

"Is there a maid or something around there?"

"Two maids. Why?"

"I just wondered. Be in the house with them when he leaves for work. Got that?"

A nod.

"And don't worry. That's the important thing. If you just take it easy there won't be a thing in the world to worry about."

I squashed my cigarette like a bug and started thinking. My mind was working now. Things were beginning to take shape. I was turning into a machine, and that made everything just that much simpler. Machines don't sweat. You throw a switch or turn a crank and the machine does what it's supposed to do. The machine named Joe Marlin was thinking now. I thought like clocks tick.

"Afterward," I said. "That's the big thing. If the hit goes properly, they won't sweat you too much. But they'll remember you. They'll list the crime as unsolved and they'll leave the file open. I can't come and move in with you the day he's in the ground. It wouldn't be too safe."

She seemed to shiver.

"The scandal will bother you," I said. "You'll stay at home awhile and then you'll go to a real estate agent. You don't want to live in Cheshire Point any more. It bothers you. You're not comfortable there any more. You just want to get away by yourself for a good long time. You can think about another house later."

"It's a nice house—"

"Just listen to me, will you? You tell him to sell the house furnished and all. Don't act hungry for money. There will be plenty of money. Tell him to list the house and take whatever he thinks is the most it'll bring. Tell him there's no rush, he should use his own judgment with the price. Then go to a travel agency and book a flight to Miami."

"Miami?"

"Right. You fly to Miami about a week after the hit. Maybe ten days at the outside. You'll have plenty of dough—insurance, loose cash. You'll go first-class, stay at the Eden Roc. You're a widow whose husband met a rather scandalous death. You want to forget about it."

"I see."

I got another cigarette going. I looked at her and I could see wheels turning inside her head. She was not a stupid woman. She would remember everything I was telling her. That was good. If she forgot, we were in trouble.

"I'll be in Miami Beach myself," I said. "I'll get a room at the Eden Roc. You see, right after the hit, I'll get the hell out of New York. Go to Cleveland, Chicago, some place like that. A week or so later I'll head for Miami. We'll be two strangers winding up at the same hotel. We won't know each other, won't arrive at the same time, won't even come from the same town. We'll meet cold and warm up. A nice relationship developing and blooming in a fast-moving resort town where relation-ships like that are no cause for comment. We'll talk, date, fall in love. Nothing will connect us with Keith or New York or anything before Miami Beach."

"A fresh start."

"You got it. From there on we do what we want. Travel, maybe. A trip around the world. Europe, the Riviera, the works. We'll have each other and we'll have a worldful of money and two lifetimes to spend it in."

"It sounds good."

"It's as good as it sounds," the machine said. "Now repeat back to me exactly what I've told you."

No tape recorder could have done it better. I heard her through, reviewed a detail or two with her, and told her she better get going. We got up from the bed and started dressing. I watched her put that virginal dress on that sensual body and felt like tearing it off again. But there would be time. Plenty of time.

I was straightening my tie in the mirror when I heard her laughing. I turned around and looked at her. She was fully dressed and she was standing close to me. I looked at the top of her head—her hair was neatly combed.

She was looking at my feet.

"What's so funny?"

She went right on laughing. I looked down and didn't get the joke. My socks matched. My shoes were good brown cordovans and I'd had a shine just a day or so ago.

She looked up and she was trying to control the laughter. I asked her once again what was so funny and she giggled.

"The shoes," she said. "You're wearing his shoes. He's still alive and already you're wearing his shoes."

I looked at the shoes, at her. She was right, of course. They were his shoes, from his suitcase. They fit perfectly and I had seen no reason to chuck them out. I stood there, a little uncertain, trying to decide how to react. Then I started to laugh, too. It was funny. We laughed until it wasn't funny any more and then I walked with her to the door.

"You'll need money," she said.

"I suppose so."

"I've been watching money since we were in Atlantic City," she said. "And I had some set aside around the house. I brought it today, almost forgot to give it to you. I don't know how long it'll last but it should be some help."

She gave me an envelope. It had his name and address in the upper left-hand corner. I made a mental note to destroy it.

"You won't call me again?"

I shook my head.

"And we won't see each other?"

"Not until it's done."

"Suppose something happens? How do I get in touch with you?"

"What could happen?"

"An emergency."

I thought about it. "No emergencies," I said. "None where getting in touch with me will do any good."

"You're afraid I'll put the police on you?"

"Don't be silly."

"Then—"

"I don't know where I'll be," I said. "And nothing

could come up, nothing where it would help to have us in contact with one another. Just do what I told you. That's all."

She shifted her weight from one foot to the other. It was an awkward moment.

"Well," she said, "I'll see you in Miami."

I nodded, awkwardly, and then I reached for her. She half-fell against me and my arms folded around her. I don't know whether the kiss was a sign of love or a bargain sealed in lipstick instead of blood. I let go of her and we stared at each other.

"Today was good," she said. "It'll be hard. Waiting a month for you."

Then she was gone. I watched her for a few seconds, then closed the door. I sat on the bed and tore the envelope open. I burned it in an ashtray, feeling slightly melodramatic, and flushed the ashes down the toilet, feeling still more melodramatic. Then I counted the money.

There was a lot of it. Over seven hundred dollars. It wasn't that much when you stopped to consider train fare to Chicago or Cleveland, then a plane to Miami. It wasn't much balanced against all the expenses I was going to run up in the next month. But it was still seven hundred dollars. It would be more than useful.

Then a thought sailed home. This was the second time Mona had given me an envelope filled with money. Both times it was shortly after we had finished making love.

That bothered me.

7.

Monday night was monotonous. I ate dinner, sat around my room at the Collingwood, and waited for time to go by. I thought about her and I thought about him and I thought about myself, and I wondered how I was going to do it. I'd made it look good for her. I'd let her think I was the boy genius with the whole routine down pat. Maybe the act set her mind to rest, but I wasn't fooling myself. I was a novice at murder.

I kept putting it together and it kept coming out wrong. My thoughts went in the usual places. I wanted to kill a man and get away with it. There are a few standard ways of doing this, and I ran them all through my head and looked for one that would fit. None of them did.

I could make it look like an accident. But the trouble with that is that there is no margin for error. When you fake an accident, or a suicide, you make one mistake and the ball game is over. One mistake and it's no longer an accident or a suicide. It's a murder, and you're it.

Cops are too good. Crime labs are too good. I could slug that fat bastard behind the ear, load him into his car and drive him over the nearest convenient cliff. Then the snoops would begin snooping. I'd leave a fingerprint somewhere, or some little punk would figure out that he'd been hit over the head before he went over the cliff, or any one of another thousand things.

Or I could get a gun, and I could stick the barrel in his fat mouth, and I could wrap his lousy hand around it and pull the trigger for him and blow his brains all over the nearest wall.

And something would be wrong, something somewhere, and somebody would know it wasn't suicide.

Then they would take Mona and they would lean on her. She'd do fine at the beginning. She'd throw it back as hard as they threw it at her.

For a while.

But they wouldn't be able to let go, because it would be murder and she would be their only suspect. They would push it as hard as they could, and she would crack before they did. Maybe she wouldn't confess, but they'd get my name out of her and pick me up, and then they would play both sides against the middle. They would scare us and make us mad, and they would break us.

They have capital punishment in New York State. They use an electric chair. In first degree murder, the chair is mandatory unless the jury recommends mercy.

They wouldn't. Not for us.

I added it up again, and each time it came out death. I worked it around again and again, over and over, and it wouldn't break properly. It wasn't fair—he had her, and he had all that money, and I wanted both of them.

There had to be a way.

I slept on it and dreamed about it. The bad dreams took up most of the night. There was an aggravating sameness about them—dreams of running, with or without Mona, running madly away and not getting away at all. We were running through a coal-black tunnel most of the time, with something very frightening chasing us and gaining on us. We would be reaching the end of the tunnel, with the darkness opening onto a pool and green grass and a picnic table, and the evilness behind us would snatch us up just as we approached the mouth of the tunnel. I never found out what the pursuer was planning to do to us, because each time, I awoke sweating at the moment of capture.

At 8:30 I got out of bed with a new angle. It was taking shape, and I sat on the edge of the bed with the day's first cigarette turning to ashes between my fingers while I let the idea play itself out. It was an intriguing idea, and it took into consideration the one salient point I hadn't stopped to consider the day before.

Brassard was a criminal.

I remembered what Mona had said. *Let's not kill him, Joe. Let's frame him and have him sent to jail.*

But that wouldn't work. I'd handed her a bucket full of all the arguments against that one. It didn't stand a chance.

Something else did. Brassard, alive, could not be

framed. Not in a million years.

Brassard, dead, was another story.

I sat there and thought it through. Every once in a while something would get tangled up and I had to start in at the beginning all over again. But all the tangles smoothed themselves out. The more I thought about it, the better it looked. When it was just about perfect I got up from the bed and went into the bathroom to shower and brush my teeth.

I sang in the shower.

I dressed in suit and tie and clean white shirt. I went downstairs and had two scrambled eggs and two cups of black coffee at the lunch counter down the street. Then I walked over to Thirty-fourth street and caught a cross-town bus to Third Avenue. The bus was crowded and I had to stand all the way. I didn't mind.

The pawnshop I was looking for wasn't the one I'd picked to hock my suitcases at. It was on Thirty-second and Third, a hole in the wall behind the inevitable three golden balls. The owner was a small, unassuming man with wire-rimmed glasses and frown lines in his forehead. His name was Moe Rader and he was a fence.

There was a kid in his shop when I walked in. The kid was trying to sell Moe a watch. I pretended to look at a saxophone while they dickered over the price. The kid settled for ten bucks, and I waited for him to take his money and go home while I wondered who the watch had belonged to, and how much it was really worth.

Then the kid was gone.

"I want a gun," I told Moe.

"Rifle or handgun or shotgun?"

"Revolver. A .38 or thereabouts."

"You have a permit, of course?"

I shook my head. He smiled sadly, showing teeth filled with gold. "If you do not have a permit, I cannot sell you a gun."

He used the tone of someone explaining an obvious fact to a very small child.

I didn't say anything.

"It's the law," he said.

I still didn't say anything. I took out my wallet and found a pair of fifties. I took them out and put them on the counter.

He looked at me, at the money, at me again. He was trying to figure out who I was.

"People," I said. "Augie Manners, Bunny DiFacio, Ruby Crane. People."

"You know these people?"

I nodded sagely.

"Tell me something about them."

I gave him the names of two night clubs that August Manners owned unofficially. I told him when Bunny DiFacio went to Dannemorra and why. I started to tell him something about Ruby Crane but he held up a hand.

"Enough," he said. "The back of the store, please."

I walked past him and into the back room. He went to the door, turned the lock, pulled down the window shade. Then he came after me, searched a shelf, produced a gun. It was a .38 revolver, Smith and Wesson. Just what I'd ordered.

"This have a history?"

He smiled the same sad smile. "Perhaps," he said. "A young boy found it in somebody's glove compartment. He brought it to me for sale. The original owner has not seen fit to report the theft to the police. We get a listing of stolen goods, you know, and I checked it carefully. I have a suspicion that this gun is not registered at all. Is that what you want to know?"

That was what I wanted to know. The gun was clean. It couldn't be traced to Moe, much less to me.

"I'll need ammunition," I said.

"A box?"

"Enough to fill the gun. Six bullets."

"You only intend to use it once?"

I didn't answer that one. He didn't really expect me to. He put half a dozen shells in a small cloth bag like the ones Bull Durham comes in. He put the bag in a little box and gave it to me.

I left the store without saying good-bye. I had a gun and six bullets and he had two fifty-dollar bills. It was that simple.

I was sitting on the edge of the bed again. The gun and the bullets nested snugly in one of my drawers in between several shirts. I was thinking again. It was getting to be a habit.

If we faked an accident, we were dead. If we faked a suicide, we were dead.

We had to fake a murder.

Respectable Westchester burghers don't get killed

often. When they do, if they are old men with young wives, it is not hard to figure out why they were killed or by whom.

But crooks are different. Crooks get killed all the time, for any number of reasons. And crooks get killed professionally. They get killed by gunmen from out of town, flown in for the job and flown out when the job is over. Gangland hits don't get solved. Gangland hits are perfect crimes. The cops don't kill themselves trying to find the killer. It would be a waste of their time.

In a sense, L. Keith Brassard was a respectable burgher. In another sense, he was a crook.

I had to kill the crook. I had to make it look like a mob hit, professionally planned and professionally carried out. I had an untraceable gun, and that was the first step.

There were other steps. But when they were done, it would be simple. It wouldn't make page three in the *Daily News*. It would be on the front page, and it would say that a Westchester gangster with a solid-gold front had been bumped by the boys. The world would leave the widow alone. They'd feel sorry for her.

They'd leave her for me.

I opened my drawer, took another look at the gun, and smiled. I closed the drawer, left the hotel, grabbed lunch. Around three that afternoon I decided to call Brassard's office and see if he was in. I looked through my wallet for his number, trying to remember whether or not I had jotted it down. I hadn't, but I had four other numbers which I stared at for several minutes. Then I remembered copying them from a slip of paper in Brassard's office.

I called them in turn from a pay phone.

The first two didn't answer. The third was a bar on the East Side in the sixties, the fourth a Greek night club in the Chelsea district. I rang off on both of them.

I guessed that the numbers were drops, contacts for Brassard's heroin business. This didn't do much for me one way or the other. It made it a little more certain Brassard was in the business, but I already knew that. I started to tear up the slip of paper, then changed my mind and returned it to my wallet.

A phone book gave me his number. I dialed WOrth 4-6363 and let it ring itself hoarse. Then I hung up and went back to my room. I used a knife blade on the lock of the attaché case and it popped open in less than a minute.

The package was still there.

I looked at it, shook a little, put it back in the case and locked it up again. I dropped my penknife into my pocket and hefted the attaché case.

I felt very shaky carrying all that heroin on the subway. But I managed it.

I got off the elevator at the fifth floor, looking very much the picture of the aspiring young businessman. My suit was pressed and my tie was straight and my attaché case was held as casually as all hell. The door was open over at Zenith Employment but nobody was looking out of it.

I let myself into Brassard's office. I closed the door behind me and looked around. The office was unchanged. I browsed around carefully. The only thing missing was the slip of paper with the four phone numbers. I thought about that one for a minute and decided to do it up brown. I found a pencil in a drawer, then got the slip from my wallet and copied the numbers on his desk pad. I came as close to his handwriting as I could remember.

Then I opened the attaché case again. I took out the small box of heroin lovingly and put it on top of the desk. Then I opened a desk drawer and took out four plain white envelopes.

I filled each of them in turn about a third of the way with heroin. I sealed them, put three in the top center drawer and wedged one into the space between the desk blotter and the leather desk set that kept the blotter in place. I let the envelope stick out a bit. Then I opened one of the bottom drawers and put the big box of heroin in the back.

That way, I figured, they'd have to look for it a little, and at the same time they couldn't help spotting it. It was sort of like a treasure hunt for little kids. The first envelope was hanging there in plain sight. No detective could possibly miss it. The other three were in the center drawer, the first place they would look. After that, of course, they would turn the office upside-down and inside-out. Then they'd find the main box and the ball game would be over.

Then the telephone started to ring.

I turned green. I backed away from the desk as though it was wired for electricity. I flattened out against the wall for no imaginable reason and counted rings.

It rang twelve times.

Somebody was trying to reach him. Somebody who was fairly sure he was there. Unless, of course, it was a wrong number. There was always that possibility. It could be a wrong number.

Then it started to ring again.

I got a quick mental picture—Brassard coming into his office any minute, finding the heroin. I got that picture and my knees started to shake. The envelopes were a nice gimmick but I couldn't risk them. I snatched the one from the desk blotter, then grabbed three more from the desk drawer. I crammed them into my pockets and prayed that he wouldn't look in the bottom drawer.

And that the cops would.

I took a look around and prayed again for salvation. Then I got out of that office and rang for the elevator.

There was a fruit juice stand across the street. I found a free stool, ordered a hot dog and a glass of pina colada, and watched the doorway to his office building. It was almost five, and I started regretting the moment of panic. I should have left the envelopes there. He wouldn't head for the office, not at this hour.

I looked down at my attaché case. No heroin, not any more. Now I had heroin in my pockets instead. A lot of it.

I worked on the hot dog and sipped the pina colada through a narrow straw. I watched the entrance, watched office girls head home from work, watched cleaning women get set for haphazard mop-up operations.

Then a cab stopped and he got out of it. He paid the

driver and the cab went away. My eyes stayed on him while he vanished into the building.

He was there for fifteen minutes.

It was a nerve-wracking, stomach-knotting quarter of an hour. On top of everything else, I had to justify my presence at the fruit juice stand by consuming two more hot dogs and two more pina coladas. Food had a tendency to stick in my throat, and it was hard.

Waiting was harder. Waiting, and wondering what he was finding, and what he was thinking, and what mistakes I had made. Waiting, and wondering where in the world to go from here. Waiting.

He came out, looking the same. I wondered if he was worried, or if I should be worried. I wondered how I was going to do it if he had discovered the boxful. There would be no way then. If my pigeon had tipped, there was only one thing to do. I had to throw up the whole thing, leave New York, forget Mona. It ought to be easy enough. I'd left many cities, forgotten many women. You just got up and went.

I remembered her, and what she was like, and what it was like to be with her. And I knew that I couldn't leave, couldn't give it up. We were in it no matter what happened.

I watched him get in a cab and go away. I finished slurping my pina colada and took a very deep breath of stale air. I walked across the street, walked into the building, rode the elevator to the fifth floor.

I jimmied the door again. It was getting tiresome. I opened the desk drawer and checked. He hadn't found the heroin. It was still there, the contents of that bottom drawer undisturbed.

A world of tension drained out of me. I reached into my pocket, rescued the four envelopes, returned them to their places. I glanced at the desk pad—the numbers weren't there any more. He'd torn up my slip of paper.

I sighed. It was a weird little game all right. I hauled out my wallet, found the slip of paper again, copied the numbers back onto the desk pad.

I played the let's-wipe-away-our-fingerprints game again, then slipped out of the office and left the building. I was beginning to think of it as my office and my building. Hell, I spent more time in it than he did.

I walked a few blocks, pitching my attaché case in a convenient trash can. I didn't need it any more. I wasn't lugging heroin around town now. It was planted properly.

A fortune in heroin. An amusing plant, I decided. An expensive investment.

I was too tired for the subway. I hailed a cab and sank back into the seat, suddenly exhausted. It had been a busy day. Too busy, maybe. I wondered how busy the next few days were going to be. Very busy, probably.

Then I thought some more about those four phone numbers. The son-of-a-bitch probably knew his own handwriting. He probably remembered tearing up those numbers once already, and he probably knew damn well that he hadn't written them the second time around. He was probably suspicious, and that was fine.

Maybe he'd push the panic button. Maybe he'd call people and let them know something was funny. That was fine, too. It would make everything else seem that more plausible.

Because no matter what happened, he wouldn't be going back to the office that night. He'd be going home to Mona. And those four little phone numbers would be around the next day.

I had to make sure that he wouldn't.

8.

After dinner I packed my suitcase and checked out of the Collingwood. I found a locker at Grand Central and shoved the suitcase into it. The gun, loaded, stayed in my inside jacket pocket. It bulged ridiculously and jiggled up and down when I walked. In the washroom of the train to Scarsdale I switched it from the jacket pocket to the waistband of my trousers. That felt a hell of a lot more professional, but it worried me. I was afraid the thing would go off spontaneously, in which case I wouldn't be much good to Mona. I tried to think about other more pleasant things.

By the time we hit Scarsdale I was beginning to shake inside. There was too much time to kill and no convenient way to kill it. I wondered whether I had taken the wrong turn. Maybe it would have been better to stay overnight at the Collingwood, then grab an early train up. That would have given me a sleepless night's sleep. But it left too much to chance. I had to pick up a car, which meant I had to hit Westchester while it was still dark out. And it was safer if I came in on a crowded train, which ruled out 4 A.M. trains. So I had picked the best way, but I still wasn't feeling too good about it.

I found a movie house a block from the train station, paid my half a buck and went in to be hypnotized. I took a seat in the back and tried to get used to the feeling of the gun in my pants. The metal wasn't cold any more. It was body temperature, or close enough, and I'd been wearing it so long it felt as though it was a part of me. I stared at the screen and let time pass.

I saw the complete show at least twice. This was not difficult. My mind couldn't stick with the picture but rambled all over the place. Even the second time through, the movie's plot sailed far over my head into the stratosphere. The movie was a thoroughly anonymous and relatively painless time-killer. It was after midnight when the last show let out and I followed the crowd out onto the empty streets of Scarsdale.

It started to get easier. The movie had turned me into the machine I had to be. Gears shifted. Buttons were pushed and switches were thrown. I found a bar—bars stay open later than movies, maybe because eyes are weaker than livers. I took a stool in the back all by myself and nursed beers until closing. Nobody talked to me. I was a loner and they were people who drank every night in the same bar. That might have been dangerous, except that they could not possibly remember me. They never noticed me in the first place.

The bar closed at four, which was fine. I went into an

all-night grill for a hamburger and a few cups of coffee. It was four-thirty almost to the minute when I left the grill, and that was just about right.

It was good weather, just beginning to turn from night to day. The air was fresh and clean, a good change from New York, with just enough of a trace of bad smells mixed with the good to keep you from forgetting that you were in the suburbs, not the country. The sky was turning light, anticipating the sun which would rise in an hour or less. There were no clouds. It was going to be one hell of a nice day.

I walked off the main street to a side street, off the side street to another side street. The neighborhood was not bad at all. It wasn't rich Scarsdale but middle Scarsdale—fairly ordinary one-family homes that cost in the mid-twenties solely because they were in Scarsdale, trees in front, hedges, the white-collar works. I had a long walk because too many people kept their cars in their garages. Then I found what I was looking for.

On the left-hand side of the street a green Mercury was parked snug against the curb. On the right-hand side there was a black Ford a year or so old. The Ford was the car I wanted. I wanted it for the same reason that the hired killer I was pretending to be would want it. It was ordinary, inconspicuous. If you are going to steal a car for a murder, you steal a black Ford. It's one of the rules of the game.

There was only one problem. The Ford's owner might wake up early. If he drove into New York every morning, he'd probably get up around seven. If he saw the car gone, and if he called the cops, the alarm for that Ford would go out before I wanted it to.

That's where the Merc came in.

I worked fast. I took the plates off the Merc, carried them to the Ford, took the plates off the Ford and put the Merc plates in their place, then crossed the street once more and put the Ford plates on the Merc. That sounds complicated—all I did, of course, was switch plates. But it would make a big difference. While the Ford owner would report his *car* missing, the Merc owner wouldn't report his *plates* missing. The chances were that he wouldn't even notice, not for a good long while. How often do you check your license plates before you get into your car?

So, even if the Ford owner reported the car stolen and some hot-shot cop checked my car, it would have different plates. Which might make a difference. Then again, it might not. But I was taking enough chances as it was. Whenever there was a chance to minimize the risk, that was fine with me.

I wiped off both sets of plates with my handkerchief, then slipped on a pair of ordinary rubber gloves, the kind they sell in drugstores. I'd bought them before I left New York, and now I was going to need them. They were good gloves—not surgical quality, but sheer enough so that my hands didn't feel like catcher's mitts. I took a good look around, prayed in silence, and opened the door of the Ford. I settled myself behind the wheel and set about jumping the ignition. It wasn't hard. It never is. I was fourteen years old when I learned how easy it was to start a car without a key. It's not the sort of thing you forget.

The car purred kittenishly. I let it scurry along to the corner. Then we took a turn and another turn and still another turn, and then we were on the main road north in the general direction of Cheshire Point. I left Scarsdale with no regrets. It was a nice place for auto theft but I would hate to live there.

The Ford was fine for murder but strictly garbage on the open road. The engine knocked gently from time to time and the pickup was several seconds behind the accelerator. The car moved like a retarded child. It was further encumbered with automatic transmission, which keeps you from shifting gears at the proper time, and power steering, which is an invention designed to drive anybody out of his mind.

I pushed the Ford along and thought about the car Mona and I would have once the whole mess was cleaned up. A Jaguar, maybe. A big sleek beast with a dynamo under the hood and an intelligent over-all approach to Newtonian mechanics, automatic division. I wondered if anybody had ever made love to her in the back seat of a Jag. I didn't think so.

Cheshire Point made Scarsdale look like Levittown. I drove around and looked at one-acre plots with half-acre mansions and smelled money. The streets were very wide and very silent. The trees lining them were very tall and very somber. It was a suburb created by expatriate New Yorkers who had fled with only their money intact, and because it was such an artificial town at the surface it was hard finding my way around. The place had very little sense to it. Streets wandered here and there, evidently intent solely on having a good time, and directions became meaningless.

I found Roscommon Drive after a struggle. It was wider than most of the streets and a parkway ran down the middle of it, a five-yard strip of shrubs and grass and greenery. I looked for house numbers, figured out where I was, and drove until I found Brassard's house. It was what I think they call Georgian Colonial. Mostly stone with white wood trim. A rolling lawn kept short and green. A large elm in the middle of the lawn. Very impressive.

I had pictured the home before. But I had never seen it, and seeing it did something to me. I gently brushed away the picture of L. Keith Brassard, Lord Of the Dope Trade, and replaced it with the illusion of complete respectability. I looked at rolling lawn and the big old elm and I saw that nice old man rolling along the Boardwalk in a rolling chair with his pretty young bride beside him. It would be fiendish to kill that man. It would be a foul, despicable crime to murder L. Keith Brassard, Pillar Of Cheshire Point.

I had to shake myself to get rid of the illusion. I had to work hard to remind myself that he wasn't a nice old man, that the fine old house was held together with needle marks and rubbery veins, that his pretty young bride was the woman I loved. I had to remind myself that he was a rotten old bastard and that I was going to murder him, and I told myself again what I had told myself a countless number of times—that the fact that he was a rotten old bastard made murdering him altogether fitting and proper.

But it was hard to believe when I looked at that house. Not the splendor of it—successful crooks live more like kings than most kings do. But the utter respectability . . .

I shook myself, more violently this time. The next step was to find the railroad station. According to Mona, he walked to the station every morning and left the car for her. That meant it was close by, and I had to figure out just how close by, and I had to know how to get there in a hurry. It would be important.

The Ford found the station; I really can't take any credit for it. The Ford nosed around until it turned up at the standard brown shed with rails running past it. Then the Ford, demonstrating a wonderful memory, found its way back to Roscommon Drive, put two and two together, and doped out the precise amount of time required to drive from the house to the station along the shortest possible route. It took about seven minutes.

It was still too early. I thought about parking in front of Brassard's house and waiting for him. I thought about Brassard looking out the window, seeing me, and coming out with a gun of his own. Then I looked around for a diner.

I found one. It had a parking lot and I nestled the Ford in it, then stripped off the gloves and pocketed them. The coffee was hot and black and strong.

I needed it.

*

I put the gloves back on later, then opened the door and slid in behind the wheel once again. If anybody had seen me I would have looked very strange to them. How often do you see a guy put on a pair of rubber gloves before he gets into his car? But nobody did, and I started the car and headed back to Roscommon Drive. It was around 8:30. He'd be working his crossword puzzle now, sitting at the breakfast table with pencil in hand and newspaper before him and cup of coffee at right elbow. I wondered if he was using the dictionary this time around, if the puzzle was hard or easy for him.

Three doors from his house I braked to a stop, plopped the Ford into neutral and pulled up the hand brake. I left the motor running. From where I sat I could see his house—the heavy oak door, the flagstone path. And, hopefully, he couldn't see me.

I wanted a cigarette. And, while I knew there was no reason in the world for me to go without that cigarette, I remembered what crime labs did with cigarette ashes. I knew it didn't matter, they could know everything there was to know about me including what brand of cigarettes I smoked and what toothpaste I used to keep my mouth kissing-sweet and whether I wore boxer shorts or briefs, and they still wouldn't be anywhere close to knowing who I was. There was nothing to link me to Brassard, nothing to make the cops think of me in the first place or second place or third place. They could have a full description of me and still get nowhere.

But I didn't smoke that cigarette.

Instead I straightened my tie, which was straight to

begin with, and studied my reflection very thoughtfully in the rear-view mirror. The mirror image was cool and calm, a study in poise. It was a lie.

I waited. And wished he would hurry up with his puzzle. And waited.

I rolled down the window on the right-hand side of the car. I opened my jacket, took out the gun. I wrapped my hand around it, curled my finger around the trigger. It was a very strange feeling, holding the gun with a glove on my hand. I could feel it perfectly, but the presence of the glove, a thin layer between flesh and metal, seemed to remove me a little from the picture of violence. The glove rather than my hand was holding the gun. The glove rather than my finger would pull that trigger.

I understood why generals didn't feel guilty when their pilots bombed civilians. And I was glad I was wearing the gloves.

8:45.

The oak door swung open and I saw him, dressed for work, briefcase tucked neatly under arm. She was seeing him to the door, looking domestic as all hell with her hair in curlers. He turned and they kissed briefly. For some reason I couldn't begrudge him that last kiss. I was almost glad he was getting the chance to kiss her goodbye. I wondered if they had made love the night before. A few days ago the thought would have sickened me. Now I didn't mind it at all. It was his last chance. He was welcome to all he could get.

She turned from him. The door closed. I released the

emergency brake and threw the car into gear.

I did not breathe while he walked down that flagstone path to the sidewalk. She would be in another room now, maybe with one of the maids. Or she would be expecting it, maybe at the window to watch in morbid fascination. I hoped she wasn't at the window. I didn't want her to watch.

He reached the sidewalk and turned away from me, heading for the railroad station. I drove up behind him. Slowly.

He walked well for a man his age. If he heard the Ford he didn't show it. One arm held the briefcase, the other swung at his side. The gun felt cold now, even with the rubber glove.

I drew up even with him, braked quickly, leaned across the seat toward him. Now he turned at the sound—not hurriedly, not scared, but wondering what was coming off. I pointed the gun at him and squeezed the trigger. Before there had been the total silence of a very quiet street. The noise of the gunshot erupted in the middle of all that silence, much louder than I had expected. I felt as though everybody in the world was listening.

I think the first bullet was enough. It hit him in the chest a few inches below the heart and he sank to his knees with a very puzzled, almost hurt expression on his face. The briefcase skidded along the sidewalk. I did not want to shoot him again. Once was enough. Once would kill him.

But the professionals don't work that way. The professionals do not take chances.

Neither did I.

I emptied the gun into him. The second bullet went into his stomach and he folded up. The third bullet was wide; the fourth took half his head off. The fifth and sixth went into him but I do not remember where.

I heaved the gun at him. Then I put the accelerator on the floor, for the benefit of any curious onlookers, and the Ford took off in spite of itself. I drove straight for two blocks with the gas pedal all the way down, then took a corner on two wheels and relaxed a little, slowing the Ford to a conservative twenty-five miles an hour.

I was sweating freely and my hands itched inside the gloves. I had to struggle to keep from speeding. But I managed it, and the ride to the station took the estimated seven minutes.

I parked the car near the station. I cut the motor, pulled up the handbrake. I stepped out of the car, closed the door, peeled off the rubber gloves and tossed them into the back seat. I wiped my hands on my pants and tried to keep calm.

Then I walked to the station. There was a newsstand on the platform and I traded a nickel for a copy of the *Times* and waited for the train to come. I had to force myself to read the headlines. Castro had confiscated more property in Cuba. There was an earthquake in Chile. No murders. Not yet.

The train came. I got on, found a seat. The car was a smoker and I got a cigarette going, needing it badly. I opened the paper to the financial pages and studied row upon row of thoroughly meaningless numbers.

I glanced around. Nobody was looking at me. Dozens of men in suits sat reading the *Times*, and none of them looked at me. Why should they?

I looked exactly the same as they did.

9.

In all of life it is the little things that stay with you. I first made love to a woman several months after my seventeenth birthday. The woman has disappeared completely from my memory. I do not know what she looked like, what her name was, only that she must have been close to thirty. Nor do I remember anything about the act. It was probably pleasurable, but I can't specifically recall pleasure and I don't think pleasure had anything to do with it. It was a barrier to be crossed, and the pleasure or lack of pleasure in the crossing was, at the time, immaterial.

But I remember something she said afterward. We were lying together—on her bed, I think—and I was telling myself silently that I was a man now. "God," she said, "that was a good one." Not *That was good* but *That was a good one*.

I must have mumbled something in the affirmative, something stupid, because I remember her laugh, a curious mixture of amusement and bitterness.

"You don't know how good it was," she said. "You're too damn young to know the difference. Young enough to do a good job and too young to know what you're doing."

I don't know what that proves, if anything. Except that the mind is a strangely selective sort of thing. The act itself should have been significant, memorable. But the act, once finished, left no impression that I can still remember. The conversation remains.

It was the same way with murder. I'm talking now about impact, not memory, but it comes out pretty much the same. I had killed a man. Killing, I understand, is a pretty traumatic thing. Soldiers and hired gunsels get used to it, sometimes, but it takes a while. I had never killed before. Now, after careful planning and deliberate execution, I had pointed a gun at a man and emptied it into him. True, he was socially worthless—a parasite, a leech—but the character of the man himself did not alter the fact that I had murdered him, that he was dead and I was his killer.

But the mind is funny. I had planned his death, I had killed him, and now it was over. Period. The simple fact of murder seemed to be something I could live with. I would not be plagued by guilt. As a result either of strength or weakness of character, I was a killer with a reasonably clear conscience.

And now the rest of it. Three things stayed with me, stuck in the forefront of my mind. The very weird expression on his face the instant before I shot him, first of all. A total disbelief, as if he had suddenly wandered into a different time-continuum where he did not fit at all.

Then there was the noise of the first gunshot. It rang so loud in my ears that the other four senses, smell and sight and taste and touch, disappeared entirely into the portion of time when the shot dominated the morning. All that sound in the middle of all that sensory silence—it was impressive.

The third thing was the utter stupidity of putting all those bullets into that very dead body. I think shooting a dead man may well be more emotionally offensive than shooting a live one. There's a concentrated brutality about it, which may explain why the newspapers and the public go wild when a murderer hacks up a corpse and stuffs it piece by piece into subway lockers, or whatever. Murder, at least, is rational. But the ridiculous mental picture of a killer emptying a gun into a man with a hole in his head is senseless, stupid, and much more terrible.

The look in a man's face. The sound of a gunshot. The waste of three or four or five bullets.

These were significant, important.

More so than murder.

The commuter train unloaded us at Grand Central. I folded the *Times* and tucked it under my arm, then followed the fold out to the lower level of the station. I was confused for a few seconds; then I got my bearings and headed for the locker where I had left my suitcase. I found it, fished out the key, unlocked the thing and picked up my bag. I carried it to the ticket office where a stoop-shouldered old man with shaggy gray hair and thick, almost opaque eyeglasses sold me a one-way coach ticket to Cleveland. The human robot at the Information Desk informed me that the next train to Cleveland left in thirty-eight minutes from Track 41. I found Track 41 without too much trouble and sat down on a bench with my suitcase between my knees.

The train was a comfortable one. It called itself the Ohio State Limited, passed through Albany and Utica and Syracuse and Rochester and Erie and Buffalo, and was due at Cleveland at 9:04 in the evening. I added thirty mental minutes to the time of arrival and settled down with my newspaper. In due course the conductor appeared, snatched my ticket and replaced it with a narrow red cardboard affair with numbers on it. He punched one of the numbers and tucked the cardboard slab into the slot on the seat in front of me. Shortly thereafter another kind gentleman made his appearance. He sold me two pieces of bread with a sliver of American cheese between them and a paper cup of orange juice to wash the sandwich down with. I handed him a dollar and he returned a nickel to me. There's nothing quite like the railroads. No other mode of transportation since the covered wagon has been able to cover such a short distance in so long a time at such a high cost. It's an accomplishment.

We hit Albany on time. We were five minutes late getting into Utica and seven more minutes behind by the time we got to Syracuse. We lost eight minutes on the road to Rochester and an additional five getting to Buffalo. Then we waited for some obscure reason in the Buffalo terminal. Maybe there was a cow on the tracks.

Something like that.

It was a quarter to ten when we made Cleveland. The train was supposed to swing south next, heading for Cinci by way of such unlikely places as Springfield and Columbus and Dayton and similar silliness, and I didn't want to think how far behind it would be when it finally made port in Cincinnati. I got off in Cleveland, suitcase in hand, and looked for a hotel and a restaurant in that order.

The hotel was at the corner of Thirteenth and Paine, rundown but respectable, reasonable but not cheap. The room had a stall shower, which helped, and a big bed which looked inviting. I changed to slightly less Madison-Avenue clothing and went out for dinner.

The restaurant was one of those let's-pretend-it's-1910 places—imitation gaslamps, sawdust on the floor, waiters with white coats and broad-brimmed straw hats. The food made up for it. I had a steak, a baked potato, a dish of creamed spinach. I drank bourbon and water before dinner, black coffee after. The coffee came in a little pewter pot with a wooden handle. What do murderers eat? What do they drink?

The Cleveland *Press* didn't have the story. It was a veritable storehouse of information about Cleveland, starting with fires and municipal corruption and finishing off with a little Conning-Towerish column of sloppy homespun-yet-sophisticated verse that almost made me throw up the steak. Here and there a reader could discover that there was a world outside of Cleveland, by George, with things happening there. There was a rocket doing something at Cape Canaveral, a revolution in Laos, an election in Italy. There was a murder in New York but the Cleveland *Press* didn't know it.

I found a trashcan to stuff the *Press* into and looked around for a newsstand that stooped to carrying New York papers. Most of them didn't. One of them did and I let him sell me the *Telly*. I took it back to the hotel, opened it up and plowed through it.

It took a lot of plowing. I started with the front page and worked toward the back, and suddenly I was on page 22 and so was the story. It filled six paragraphs in the third column and was topped neatly by a two-deck eighteen point head that read like so:

MAN SHOT DEAD OUTSIDE
HOME IN WESTCHESTER

Gunfire shattered the early-morning calm today in residential Cheshire Point when five bullets fired from a moving car felled a prominent importer steps from his own door.

The victim was Lester Keith Brassard of 341 Roscommon Drive, 52-year-old importer with offices in lower Manhattan. He was killed as he left his home for his office. Local police recovered a stolen car, believed to be the murder vehicle, several blocks from the scene of the crime.

Mona Brassard, the victim's wife, was unable to advance any information as to a possible motive for the slaying, conducted in typical gangland fashion. "Keith didn't have an enemy in the world," she told police and reporters. She admitted that he had seemed nervous lately. "But it was something about business," she said. "He didn't have any personal problems. None that I knew about."

Arnold Schwerner, detective on the Cheshire Point police force, agreed that the slaying seemed pointless. "He could have been hit by mistake," he theorized. "It looks like a pro job."

Schwerner's statement was in reference to the method of murder—several shots from a stolen car. This method has been in vogue among gangsters for years.

Cheshire Point police are working on the killing in close cooperation with detectives attached to Manhattan's Homicide West.

The last paragraph was the kicker. If Homicide West was tied in already, that meant the cops were looking for a business motive for the murder. That, in turn, meant that the office would get some sort of going-over. I couldn't be positive they'd hit the heroin, but the odds were long that they would. Homicide West is by no means a lousy outfit.

I re-read the part where they quoted Mona and I couldn't help grinning like a ghoul. She had carried it off perfectly, hitting just the right tone. *Keith didn't have an enemy in the world*—except for his lovely wife and her boyfriend. *He seemed a little nervous lately. But it was something about business. He didn't have any personal problems. None that I knew about.*

The right tone. She hadn't tried to explain things for them, but had given them a few hints and let them reconstruct it for themselves. I'd staged the job right—a slaying conducted in typical gangland style. Now she had reacted properly, and the heroin was the next link in the chain. When they found that, the ball game was over. That made it a gangland slaying, all right. What the hell else could it be?

I folded the newspaper and put it in the wastebasket. Then I set a cigarette on fire and found a chair to sit in. I wanted to get some plans made, but it wasn't easy. I kept seeing that look of total disbelief on the face of Lester Keith Brassard. I hadn't known his name was Lester. It explained why he preferred Keith. So would anybody in his right mind.

I would see the face, and I would hear the shot. Then I would see myself stretched across the front seat of that black Ford pumping bullets into a corpse. According to the papers, the police thought the car was moving at the time. That was fine with me. That meant two killers, one firing the gun and the other handling the driving. The crime lab could probably figure out that it hadn't happened that way, but by that time it would be a moot point. For the time being, let them figure on two killers. Or five. Or a damned platoon.

The face, and the shot, and the exercise in studied stupidity. They paraded in front of me, and I wondered if maybe this was what they meant by guilt. Not sorrow for the act, not a feeling that the act was wrong, not even a fear of punishment—but a profound distaste for certain memories of the act, certain sensory impulses that lingered persistently.

I don't think Brutus was sorry that he knifed Caesar. I don't think he thought it was wrong.

But I am positive the line *Et tu, Brute* haunted him until he ran upon the sword that Strato held for him. That line would do it for him, just as the blood did it for Macbeth and his good wife.

I lighted another cigarette and tried to think straight. It was not easy.

According to plan, she would leave for Miami a week to ten days after the murder. It was Wednesday now, Wednesday evening, and by the Saturday after next she would be at the Eden Roc. I had told her I would be there before her. I could leave any time.

The funny part of it was that I didn't entirely want to. I had been a machine, oiled and primed for the murder, and now that it was over and done with I felt functionless. I was through. The easy part remained, but I didn't even want a hand in the easy part of it. A weird thought nagged at me. I had better than five hundred bucks left. I could pack up and go—find a new town, use the dough for a fresh start. I could forget all that woman and all that money.

And the face and the noise and the five useless bullets.

It was an emotional reaction to murder, not sensible, not logically considered. It wasn't logical because then I would have killed L. Keith Brassard for nothing at all. The spoils belonged to the victor. I had won, and now Brassard's wife and Brassard's money were mine to keep.

Both were desirable. It would be idiotic to turn down either of them.

It came out the same way if you looked at the emotional set-up piece by piece. I still loved Mona, still wanted her, still needed her. Even if I had the money, I was nowhere without her. She made the difference. She was the New Life, the Higher Purpose, all of that crap.

I had to laugh. A face and a noise and five extra bullets sat on one side. Mona and money were perched on the other. The choice was so simple, so obvious, that there really was no choice. I'd be in Miami by Saturday and she'd be there four or five days after that.

I ground out my cigarette, glad that all that nonsense was settled. The air outside was heavy with industrial smoke and human perspiration. I forced myself through it, found a bar, had a drink. A whore sat there waiting for me to pick her up. The impulse was suddenly strong; the desire for a magical release from all that tension was tough to resist. I looked at her and she smiled, showing at least fifty-three teeth, none of them hers to start with.

She was the kind of woman who looks fine if you don't get too close. A hard, tough body built for action. A face camouflaged with too much of every cosmetic known to modern woman. Cheap clothes cheaply worn. And I remembered the line from Kipling: *I've a neater, sweeter maiden in a cleaner, greener land.*

I turned away from her and paid attention to my drink. I finished it, scooped up my change and walked away from Mandalay. I thought about a movie and decided I really didn't have the strength to sit through one. They were good time-killers, but enough is enough. Maybe someday I would be able to go to a movie because I wanted to go to a movie. Maybe someday I would be able to go to a movie and watch the damn thing.

But not for a while.

I walked around for a few more minutes, maybe half an hour altogether. I passed movie theaters, passed bars that I didn't bother entering. I wandered past the Greyhound station and again the impulse came, the urge to get on the first bus and go wherever it went. With my luck it would have gone to New York.

More walking. Then it occurred to me that, for one thing, I was dog-tired, and, for another, I had absolutely nothing to do. The obvious course of action involved going back to my hotel and hitting the sack. But I knew instinctively that I wouldn't be able to fall asleep for hours. After all, I had recently finished committing a murder. You do any of several things after committing a murder, and falling asleep with ease is not one of them. It only stood to reason that, this being my first homicide to date, it would be sunrise before I could start thinking seriously about something like sleep.

I decided not to be logical. The sleepy clerk tossed me my key and the sleepy elevator operator ran me up to my floor. I felt a kinship for both of them. I got out of my clothes, washed up, and crawled under the covers.

I got all ready to count sheep. The sheep were little naked Monas and they did not look like sheep at all. They were only woolly here and there, and they were not built much like sheep. Nor were they jumping over a fence.

Instead they leaped gaily over a corpse. You know who *he* was.

By the time the fourth Mona got over the corpse, I had gotten over my insomnia. I slept like a corpse, and nobody jumped over me.

10.

I made the front page of the Times. Not the lead story, which was devoted to the names somebody called somebody else in the Security Council of the United Nations. Not even the second lead, which was devoted to some new invention in the realm of municipal corruption. But, by Times standards, I got a big play—ten inches of copy set double-column in the left-hand corner of page one. That's the equivalent of the front-page banner in the News or Mirror, which I found out later, I also made.

The headline on the Times story read: NARCOTICS CONNECTION SEEN LIKELY IN CHESHIRE POINT MURDER. As is generally the case with *New York Times* headlines, that turned out to be the understatement of the year. The story, with ten inches of copy on the front page and fifteen more on page 34, made everything very nice indeed. I couldn't have asked for anything more.

Homicide West had located the heroin after what the *Times* graciously referred to as "a meticulous scrutiny of

Brassard's offices at 117 Chambers Street." I didn't see any need for meticulous scrutiny—not with an envelope of heroin sticking out from under a desk blotter and three more in the top drawer. But I didn't want to quarrel with the *Times*.

The cache of heroin, according to the *Times*, had a retail value in excess of a million dollars. What in the world that meant was anybody's guess. By the time the stuff was retailed it would have passed through the hands of fifteen middlemen and would have been cut as many times. The retail value was pretty much irrelevant, and there was no way of figuring out what the wholesale value of the stuff might have been. Nor did it matter much, when you stopped to think about it.

From there on, naturally, they had put two and two together. And, naturally, had come up with four. The phone numbers, said the *Times*, were those of several well-known narcotics drops. Why they were still open if they were known as narcotics drops was neither asked nor answered. What with the dope and the numbers, and a meticulous scrutiny of Brassard's books, Homicide had managed to figure out that Lester Keith Brassard was an importer of more than cigarette lighters.

This fact, coupled with the mode of murder employed, made the final conclusion inevitable. Brassard had been bumped by racket boys, either because he had crossed them or because they wanted to move in on his operation. The *Times* reporter, who had obviously seen a few too many movies about the Mafia, thought this might be an aftermath of the Appalachian meeting, with the mob moving out of the drug trade. According to this interpretation, poor Lester Keith was a high-ranking mobster who refused to go along with the shift in policy and had suffered the consequences of "bucking the syndicate." It was a pretty fascinating theory and a marvelous example of interpretative journalism in action. I hoped the kid would cop himself a Pulitzer for it.

There were three or four paragraphs about Mona in the story and they all said just what I wanted them to say. The distraught widow was completely taken aback by the new developments in the case. Any intimation that her husband was less than a solid citizen shocked the marrow from her bones. Of course she had never been quite clear on what he did for a living. He wasn't the sort of man who brought his business home from the office. He made a good living, and that was as much as she knew. But she just couldn't *believe* that he would be mixed up in something . . . something actually *criminal*. Why, it just wasn't like Keith at all!

She should have been an actress.

I liked that article. What it left out was as important from my point of view as what it included. The Cheshire Point side of the case had disappeared almost completely. A few witnesses had popped out with the usual mutually conflicting stories. One insisted the three killers had called out *This is for Al, you bastard* before shooting. The rest came a little closer to reality, but not a hell of a lot. The important part was that nobody seemed to give a damn about the shooting itself any more. Brassard, unmasked as a scoundrel, would not be mourned. The police, busy chasing down narcotics leads, wouldn't care about the killing as such. Mona would be left alone, except for the sob-sister reporters whom she'd quite justifiably refused to speak to. Nobody would be especially surprised when she put the house up for sale and headed for Florida to get away from it all. Nor would anybody take much notice when she married me four or five months later, on the rebound, so to speak. It would be perfectly consistent, and that was the important thing. Consistency. You can build a whole world of lies, as long as each lie reinforces every other lie. You can create a masterful structure of sheer logic if you begin with one false postulate. All it takes is consistency.

That night I saw a movie. The whole day up to that point had been unreal. It was a waiting time and nothing was happening. I felt only partially alive, hibernating without being able to sleep. The total lack of eventfulness was overpowering, especially after a time of planning and a time of acting and a time of running. So this time the movie was not a time-killer but a vicarious experience, an attempt to replace my own passiveness with the activity of the celluloid images.

Perhaps this is why I watched the movie more closely than I would have normally. It was a Hitchcock film, an old one, and it was gripping. The switches from tension to comedy, from the terrifying to the ridiculous, were amazingly effective. But for a change I saw past the surface to the plot itself, and I saw that the plot was ludicrous—a web of preposterous coincidences held together by superior writing and acting and directing.

Later, lying in bed and trying to sleep, I realized something. I tried to imagine a movie in which the hero steals two pieces of luggage, one of which is loaded with a fortune in raw heroin. Then the same hero happens to pick up or get picked up by a girl who subsequently turns out to be the wife of the guy who owns the luggage and the heroin.

Coincidental?

More than that. Almost incredible. At least as far-fetched as the picture—and yet I had been able to accept coincidence in life simply because it had happened to me. The fictional coincidences in the Hitchcock film were different. They had not happened in life, but only on the screen.

It was something to think about. I had never looked at it quite that way before, and I spent a little time running it through my mind.

"Would you care for a magazine, sir?"

I shook my head.

"Coffee, tea, or milk?"

I shook my head again. The stewardess, as pretty and as faceless as Miss Rheingold, wandered off to bother somebody else. I looked out the window at the ground and saw clouds instead. They look very different from above. When you fly over them they are not white puffballs of cotton at all, just shapeless, moderately dense fog. I stared at them for a few more seconds, but they didn't do a hell of a lot to hold my interest. I looked away.

It was Saturday morning. The plane was a jet, flying direct to Miami, and we would be landing a few minutes past noon. The night before, I had phoned the Eden Roc and reserved a single; it would be waiting for me. That was a piece of luck. There was a time when Miami Beach was empty in the summer. Now the summer season is as busy as the winter one, although the prices are a good deal lower.

"Attention please."

I listened to the male voice come over the loudspeaker and wondered what was wrong. I remembered that I was on a plane, and that periodically planes crashed for the sheer hell of it. I wondered, quite calmly, whether we were going to crash.

Then the same voice—the pilot's—went on to tell me that we were cruising at an altitude of so many feet, that the temperature in Miami was such-and-such, that landing conditions were ideal and that we were destined to arrive on time. The pilot closed with a message advising me to select his airline for future flights and I thought what an idiot I was. We were not going to crash. All was well.

We landed on time, happily. I got off—the stewardess called it *deplaning*, a cunning word—and wandered away to wait for my luggage in the terminal. The sun was hot and the sky was cloudless. Good Florida weather, good beach weather. Mona and I could lie on the beach and soak up the sun. We could lie on the beach at night and soak up the moonlight, too. I remembered Atlantic City, the first time, on the beach at midnight. Life is a circle.

The luggage got there after ten minutes or so and I traded my baggage check for it, then carried it to the waiting limousine which would cruise northward to Miami Beach. The tall, rangy driver was a native of the state. There were two ways to tell—his speech, which sounded more like Kentucky or Tennessee than Deep South. Dade County natives have that hill inflection nine times out of ten. The other tip-off was his total lack of a suntan. The people who live in Miami know enough to stay out of the sun. Only the Yankee tourists are sun-worshippers. He was also a good driver. He made fine time, dropping me at my hotel sooner than I'd expected. A bellhop snatched my bags and I followed him to the front desk. Yes, they had my reservation. Yes, my room was ready for me. And welcome to the Eden Roc, Mr. Marlin. Right this way, sir.

I was on the fifth floor, a big single with a huge bathroom and a view of the ocean. I looked out the window and saw browned bodies dotting a golden beach. The sea was very calm—no surf at all, gently rippling waves. I watched a gull swoop for a fish, watched one little kid chase another little kid along the edge of the shore, watched two college-boy-types burying a college-girl-type with sand. Miami Beach.

The beach was pleasant that afternoon, the sun warm, the water refreshing. I stayed out until it was time for dinner. The crowd thinned out as the day wore away. Fat middle-aged men from New York rubbed sunburn cream on themselves, changed into loud sportclothes and went to play gin rummy on the terrace. Mothers herded children back to their rooms. The sun went away.

After dinner I caught the floorshow. The headliner was a busty female singer who was even worse in person than she was on records. But the comic was amusing and the band passable. Drinks were expensive. I wasn't worried. When the time came to settle the tab, Mona would be on hand with half the money in the world. No sweat in that department.

That was Saturday. Sunday was about the same, and Monday and Tuesday. My tan deepened and my muscles loosened up from all the swimming. Monday afternoon I spent awhile in the gym, working out gingerly. Then I went to the steamroom and sweated. A big Pole without a hair on his head massaged me for fifteen minutes and left me feeling like a new man. I had never been in better physical shape.

I drank the nights away, always getting slightly high and never taking on too much of an edge. I kept turning down chances to sleep with the wives of other men. The need for a woman was strong, and the women were startlingly available, but one trick never failed me. I would look at them and compare them with Mona. They never came close.

Wednesday I started to expect her. I spent most of the afternoon in the lobby, my eyes flashing to the desk every ten minutes or so. It was a full week since the murder and she would be around any time from then on. There were no complications. The murder was getting very little play in the New York papers—a few inches in a back page of the *Times* now and then, nothing much else. I waited for her.

When she didn't show on Thursday I got impatient. After all, I had told her a week, ten days tops. And with everything running so smoothly she didn't have to waste any time. All was clear. To hell with cloaks and daggers, Mitchum in a trenchcoat. I wanted my woman.

She didn't show Friday, either.

I drank too much Friday night. I sat in front of the bar and poured too many shots of straight bourbon down my throat. It could have been dangerous, but I became a silent drunk instead of a noisy one, which was fortunate. A bellhop poured me into bed and I woke up early with a brand-new hangover. There was a wire running through my head from one ear to the other. It was red hot and somebody was strumming it. A Bloody Mary made things a little better. Only a little.

Saturday morning. A full week of Miami Beach, which is plenty. And no Mona. I waited all day long in the lobby and she did not show up.

I started to sweat. I almost walked over to the desk to ask if she had a reservation, which would have been a new experiment in stupidity. Instead I went outside and walked down Collins to the first bar. It had a pay phone and I used it to call the Eden Roc. I asked for Mrs. Brassard.

"One moment," the clerk said. I waited more than a moment and he came back again.

"I'm sorry," he said. "But we have no one staying here under that name."

"Could you check the reservations?"

He could, and he did. There were no reservations

for Mrs. Brassard, either.

I went to the bar and had a drink. Then I went back and tried to straighten myself out. Maybe she forgot which hotel to stay at, or maybe the Eden Roc was full, or something. I made half a dozen calls. I checked the Fontainebleau and the Americana and the Sherry Frontenac and the Martinique and two other places I no longer remember. Each time I asked first for Mrs. Brassard, then asked if she had a reservation there. Each time I drew a blank.

There was an answer, somewhere. There had to be. But whatever it was, I couldn't figure it out. I was looking at things wrong, or things were happening wrong, and I felt like a rat in a maze. They have a cute little ploy at the psychology laboratories. They take a rat that's been taught to solve mazes and they put him in a maze with no way out. The rat tries everything and nothing works. Then, inevitably, the rat reacts to all this frustration by sitting in a corner and chewing off his feet.

I didn't chew off my feet. I went back to the Eden Roc and took a cold shower and thought about the bill that was going to fall due any day. I wondered if I'd be able to cover it. And I wondered how long it would take her to show up. The only answer was that she hadn't bothered with a reservation. Maybe she had had to stay in New York until the estate was settled. You read about things like that. Legal problems that can tie you up for a while. Little things.

I told myself that story until I believed it. And the night came and went, and the next morning I hit the beach and let the sun bake a lot of bitterness and anxiety out of me. I swam and slept and ate and drank and that was Sunday.

I was up late Monday morning. I went to breakfast, which they serve at the Eden Roc until three P.M., and then I headed for the elevator.

The clerk was too quick for me.

"Mr. Marlin—"

I could have pretended not to hear him. But the bill was going to get to me sooner or later and there was no particular point in dodging it for a day or so. I could probably cover it anyway. So I went over to the desk and he smiled at me.

"Your statement," he said, handing me a folded hunk of yellow paper. I showed him I could be just as polite as he was and put it in my pocket without looking at it.

"And a letter," he added. He gave it to me. It must have been a reflex, because I put that one in my pocket without looking at it, and this was not easy.

"Thanks," I said.

"Do you know how long you'll be staying with us, Mr. Marlin?"

I shook my head. "Hard to say," I said. "Nice place you've got here. Enjoyable."

He beamed.

"Few more days," I said. "Maybe a week. Might even be two weeks. Then again, I might have to leave on a moment's notice. Hard to say."

The smile remained. It seemed rude to walk away in the middle of such a nice smile but he held it so firmly that he left me no choice. I let him smile across the lobby while I rode upstairs in the elevator.

First the statement. It was a honey, and it scared me. It came to an impressive $443.25. More than I'd figured. Too many days, too much good food, too much liquor. I didn't *have* $443.25.

I folded the yellow paper back on the original folds and made a place for it in my wallet. Then I took out the envelope and turned it over and over in my hands like a child trying to guess the contents of a birthday present. It was thick. No return address.

I opened it.

There was a sheet of plain white paper. It was the wrapper. It held money.

Money.

Hundred-dollar bills.

I counted them, thinking how immaterial the hotel bill had suddenly become. There were thirty of them, each crisp and fresh and new, each a hundred. Thirty hundred-dollar bills. Thirty hundred dollars. Three thousand dollars.

A lot of money.

And all the worry drained out of me, because I knew that there was no longer anything to worry about. Mona had not forgotten I was alive. The estate was not tied up—not if she could ship me three grand in cash.

There were no problems.

I hefted the money. It was more than cash—it was a symbol. It meant very definitely that everything was all right now, no worry, no sweat. God was in His heaven and all was right with the world. It was her way of telling me this—an apology for her tardiness and a promise that she would be around soon. I felt myself growing warm at the thought of her. Soon, I thought. Very soon. Very, very soon.

She had gotten tied up. Well, that sort of thing could happen. And she couldn't chance a letter or a phone call or a wire. She had trusted me to wait for her, and now she was making sure that I knew all was well. I felt guilty suddenly for worrying. It had been rotten of me.

But I would make it up to her.

She was in New York now. But soon—any day now—she would be on her way to Miami.

Any day.

First things first. I put on swim trunks, threw a towel over my shoulders and picked the top six bills off the roll. I put the rest in the wallet and popped the wallet into the dresser drawer. I looked around for the wastebasket, then changed my mind and flipped the envelope in the drawer too.

In Miami Beach you can take an elevator to the lobby in your bathing suit. The only formal part of the place is the financial end of things. And I was taking care of that now.

The clerk had the same smile on his face.

"Might as well get this out of the way," I told him. And I pushed five hundred dollars across the desk.

"You hang onto the change," I went on, feeling richer than God. "Put it on my account. Just one pocket in these trunks and it's too damn small to be much good."

I walked across the lobby to the beach entrance and felt seven feet tall and eight feet wide. It was Chamber of Commerce weather again and I was in the right mood for it. I found a spot to dump my towel, then ran straight into the ocean. The waves were higher than they had been and I dived right into the middle of one. It felt great.

A funny-faced man with a very deep tan and a very large stomach was teaching his little daughter how to swim. He held his hand out, palm up, and she had her stomach on it while she flailed the water madly with her arms and kicked furiously with two small pink feet. I grinned at her and at him and felt happy.

I swam around some more. I went over to the terrace and had a vodka collins. I stretched out on my towel and let the sun bake the vodka out again.

It was a good thing I already had a pretty deep tan, because I fell asleep there with the sun going full blast. It was a nice way to fall asleep. There was all that warmth, and there was my head dancing with memories of Mona and thoughts about Mona and nice things like that. There was a cool breeze off the ocean and the pleasant babble of kids and an occasional skywriting plane droning away over the ocean.

So I slept.

The sun was gone when I woke up. So was the heat— the beach was cold and I was chilly. I wrapped up in the towel and headed for my room.

The funny part of it was that a lot of the pleasant glow of well-being had set with the sun. Now, oddly, something seemed to be wrong, which was ridiculous. I shook myself angrily, not even amused this time around. What the hell—I'd drifted off to sleep dreaming happy dreams, and I'd gotten up feeling troubled again.

What was it? The face and the noise and the five bullets? I still thought about them, once in a while, whenever I drank a little too much.

But that wasn't it.

Something else.

I let myself into my room, found a fresh pack of cigarettes and got one going. The smoke didn't taste good but I smoked anyway, nervously, and ground the cigarette out with half of it still to go. What was wrong?

I walked over to the dresser, opened the drawer. I took out my wallet and looked at all that wonderful green paper that had come all the way from New York. I looked at the plain envelope it had come in.

Maybe I saw it before. You can do that—see things and not notice them consciously. They stick with you, deep in your mind, and they nag at you.

Or maybe I was psychic.

Or maybe something just smelled wrong. Maybe something didn't add up no matter how nice I made it sound. Maybe a few hours in the sun made up for the rationalization and let the bad smell reveal itself.

I looked at that plain envelope from New York. I looked at it until my eyes bulged.

It was postmarked Las Vegas.

11.

We made love in my room at the Shelburne. Then, while I was lying on my bed in the dark smelling the last traces of her perfume, the door had opened less than six inches. An envelope fell to the floor and the door closed at once.

That envelope had contained three hundred seventy dollars.

We made love in my room at the Collingwood. Just before she left she gave me an envelope. That one had contained somewhat better than seven hundred dollars. Maybe my performance was better that time, or maybe stud service gets increasingly more profitable as you go along.

This time the pay was three grand and I hadn't even made love to her.

Now I remembered the bad feeling at the Collingwood after she gave me the money. The weird feeling that the money was a payment for services rendered. That was obviously what the three grand constituted—payment, probably in full, for the removal of her husband. I wondered what the market price was for husbandicide. Or was there a set price? Maybe it varied, because there were plenty of variables that deserved consideration. The net worth of the husband, for example, and the comparative misery of living with him. Those were important factors. It ought to cost more to kill an obnoxious millionaire than to bump a good-natured and uninsured pauper. It only stood to reason.

Three thousand dollars for murder.

Three thousand dollars.

Three thousand dollars and not even a note that said *good-bye*. Three thousand dollars and not a word, not a return address, nothing. Three thousand dollars as a kiss-off, with a plain envelope plainly saying *It's over, you're being paid for everything, go away and forget me and to hell with you*. Three thousand dollars' worth of very cold shoulder.

With three thousand dollars you can buy two hundred thousand cigarettes. I smoke two packs of cigarettes a day. Three thousand dollars would keep me in cigarettes, then, for almost fourteen years. With three thousand dollars you can buy four hundred fifths of good bourbon, or one fairly good new car, or three hundred acres of very cheap land. With three thousand dollars you can buy thirty good suits, or one hundred pairs of good shoes, or three thousand neckties. You can shoot pool for six thousand consecutive hours if you want.

Three thousand dollars for murder.

It was not nearly enough.

What surprised me was the strange calm that had come over me, probably because the full impact hadn't reached me yet. I was seeing everything in a different light—Mona, myself, the whole picture of the curious little game we had played. I was her pigeon all the way down the line. I killed for her, more for her than for the money. I ran to Miami and waited for her, and she ran to Vegas and forgot me.

But why pay me at all?

Not as a sop to her conscience, because I knew full well she didn't have one. Not to even things out, because three thousand dollars was hardly a fair share.

Why?

I thought about it, and I came up with two answers that seemed to fit. One of them was sensible enough. Without some kind of word from her, I'd panic. I'd wonder where she was and I'd try to get in touch with her. Eventually I'd find some way to bollix things up. She didn't want that to happen, so she had to let me know I was being brushed off. Her way was perfect—no note, no call, no wire. Just properly anonymous money.

The other answer could make sense only to Mona. She was a girl who was used to having things break right with her. Maybe, if she gave me a little piece of change, I would go away and disappear. Maybe I'd be happy with my tiny cut and leave her alone. Maybe I'd take the dough, given to me out of the goodness of her heart, and skip with it. Wishful thinking. But Mona was a wishful person.

Three thousand dollars. I could forget all about her

with three thousand dollars. I could use the money to cruise Miami Beach good and hard until I found myself a rich divorcee and parlayed her into a life-long meal-ticket. I could buy a fresh start with three grand, and that was what she was counting on me to do.

She didn't know me at all.

Somehow the thought of sea and surf had lost its charm for me. So had the thought of food. But the bar was open, and liquor was far from unattractive. I drank but did not get drunk. I was too busy listening to small voices located somewhere deep inside my brain. They did not stop talking.

I think I would have been able to forget her if the money had been the main thing. But it hadn't. I shot holes in Keith Brassard because I wanted his wife, not his money. And I had been double-crossed not by a temporary partner in crime but by the potential reward of the crime itself. Two things—I couldn't let her get away with it. And I couldn't let her get away from me.

I drank bourbon and thought about murder. I thought of ways to kill her. I thought of guns and knives. I looked at my hand, fingers wrapped tight around an old-fashioned glass, and I thought of barehanded murder. Strangling the life out of her, beating the life out of her. I drank some more bourbon and remembered a face and a noise and five bullets, and I knew that I was not going to kill her.

For one thing, I was certain I could never kill anybody again. The thought came to me, and I accepted it at once as gospel, and then I began to wonder why it was so. Not because killing Brassard had been difficult, or frightening, or even dangerous. But because I did not like killing. I didn't know whether or not that made sense and I didn't care. I knew it was true. That's all that really mattered.

I was not going to kill her. Because I did not want to kill, and also because that would not solve anything. There would be a risk for no reward but revenge. I would get vengeance, but I would not get that money and I would not get Mona.

I still wanted the money. And I still wanted the woman. Don't ask me why.

"Do you have a match?"

I had a match. I turned and looked at the girl who wanted a match. Brunette, mid-twenties, chic black dress and good figure. Dark lipstick on her mouth, a cigarette drooping from her lips, waiting for a light. She didn't want a match.

I lighted her cigarette. She was poised and cool but not at all subtle. She leaned forward to take the light and to give me a look at large breasts harnessed by a lacy black bra. Eve learned that one the day they got dressed and moved out of Eden. It has been just as effective ever since.

I remembered the whore in Cleveland and the snatch of song from Mandalay. I paraphrased it now in my mind: *I've a richer, bitchier maiden in a funny money land.* Mona was rich and a bitch and in Vegas. Bad verse but accurate.

The *neater sweeter* routine was an empty dream. The girl on the stool beside me was pretty. I didn't have to pretend I was a priest any more.

I returned her smile. I caught the bartender's eye and pointed meaningfully at her empty glass. He filled it.

"Thank you," she said.

The conversation was easy because she did all of it. Her name was Nan Hickman. She played jockey to a typewriter for a New York insurance company. She had two weeks' vacation. The rest of the stenos used their two weeks to hunt a husband in the Catskills. She didn't like the Catskills and she didn't want a husband. She wanted to have fun but she wasn't having any.

She was sweet and warm and honest. She was not cheap. She wanted to have fun. In two weeks she would go back to the Bronx and turn into a pumpkin. Her mother would know who she went out with and when she came in. Her aunts would try to find husbands for her. She only had two weeks.

I put my hand on her arm. I looked at her and she didn't look away.

"Let's go upstairs," I said. "Let's make love."

I left change on the bar. We went upstairs, to her room, and we made love. We made love very slowly, very gently, and very well. She'd been drinking something with rum in it and her mouth tasted warm and sweet.

She had a good body. I liked the way her body was pale white from her breasts to her thighs and tan on arms and legs and face. I liked to look at her and I liked to touch her, and I liked to move with her and against her. And afterward it was good to lie next to her, hot and sweaty and magnificently exhausted, while the earth shifted slowly back into place.

For a while there was no need to talk. Then there was, and she said little things about herself and about her job and about her family. She had an older brother, married and Long Islanded, and younger sister.

She didn't tell me that she was the closest thing in the world to a certified virgin. She didn't apologize for picking me up and sleeping with me. She wanted to have fun.

And she didn't talk about tomorrow, or the day after tomorrow, or the days after that. She didn't talk about home or family or marriage or little white houses with green shutters. Nor did she ask me any questions.

I looked at her pretty face, at her breasts and belly. I thought what a good thing it would be to fall in love with her and marry her. I wished I could do just that and knew that I couldn't.

I've a richer, bitchier maiden . . .

I waited until she was sleeping. Then I slipped out from under the sheet and got dressed. I didn't put on my shoes. I did not want to wake her.

I looked down at her. Some day somebody would marry her. I hoped he would be good enough for her, and that they would be happy. I hoped their children would look like her.

I walked out, holding my shoes in one hand, and went back to my room.

°

After breakfast the next morning I checked out of the Eden Roc. The desk clerk was sorry to see me go. Sorry or not, the smile never left his face.

He checked my account. "You have a refund coming, Mr. Martin. A little over thirty dollars."

"Tell you what," I said. "Didn't have a chance to leave anything for the chambermaid. Why don't you hang onto the money, spread it around here and there?"

He was surprised and pleased. I wondered how much of the money would stick to his fingers. I didn't care. I didn't need the thirty-odd dollars and it didn't make any difference to me who got it.

Surprisingly few things made any difference to me.

I found a phone booth at a bar—not the same one I had used before but pretty much the same. It was a complex proposition. I called Cheshire Point Information and asked for the largest realtor. I got through to his office and asked if 341 Roscommon Drive was on his list. It wasn't. Could he find out who had it? He could, and would call me back collect. I waited.

I had never before had the experience of accepting a collect call in a pay phone. The operator ascertained that it was really me on the line, then told me to throw money into the machine. I did.

"Lou Pierce has the property on the board," he told me. "Pierce and Pierce." He gave me their number and I jotted it down.

"High asking price," he said. "Too high, if you ask me. I can give you the same sort of property, same neighborhood, maybe five thousand dollars cheaper. Good terms, too. You interested?"

I told him I didn't think so but I'd let him know. I thanked him and told him he'd been a big help. Then I rang off, threw another dime in the hole and got the operator. I put through a call to Pierce and Pierce and got somebody named Lou Pierce on the phone almost immediately.

"Fred Ziegler called me," he said. "Told me you've got your eyes on the 341 Roscommon Drive place. Believe me, you couldn't do better. Beautiful home, lovely grounds. A bargain."

I almost told him Ziegler had said different but checked the impulse. "I've seen the property," I said. "I'm not interested in buying. I'd like some information."

"Oh?"

"About Mrs. Brassard."

"Go ahead," he said. Part of the warmth was gone and his voice sounded guarded.

"Her address."

There was a pause, a brief one. "I'm sorry," he said, not sounding all that sorry at all. "Mrs. Brassard left strict instructions to keep her address confidential. I can't give it out. Not to anybody."

That figured.

I was prepared for it. "Oh," I said, "you don't understand. She wrote to me herself, told me where she was staying. But I lost her Nevada address."

He was waiting for me to say more. I let him wait.

"She wrote you, huh? Told you where she was staying, but you lost the letter?"

"That's right."

"Well," he said. "Well. Look, I'm not saying I don't believe you. Seems to me if somebody wrote me the name of a hotel in Tahoe it wouldn't go out of my head, but I got a better memory than a lot of people. But all I can do is what she told me. I can't go giving out confidential information."

He already had.

I put up a minor bitch to preserve appearances. Then I acknowledged his position, thanked him anyway, and hung up on him. I hoped the conscientious objectionable didn't realize how many beans he had spilled.

I picked up my bags, left the bar and found a cab to dump them into. I climbed in after them and sat down, heavily.

But I lost her Nevada address.

It must have been luck, saying Nevada instead of Vegas. I'd been angling for the address itself, not the name of the town. Somehow the possibility that she might mail the letter out-of-town hadn't occurred to me. I'd been hunting the address, and I hadn't gotten it. Now I didn't need it any more.

Tahoe. Not Vegas. Good old Lake Tahoe, where I had never been in my life. But I knew a little about Tahoe. I knew it was small enough so that I could find her with ease whether I knew the name of her hotel or not.

Tahoe.

And I got another part of the picture, a picture of Mona Brassard throwing dice in a posh club in Tahoe and laughing her head off about the poor clod searching all over Vegas for her. It made a funny picture.

She would be surprised to see me.

They didn't have a direct flight to Lake Tahoe. TWA had one to Vegas with one touchdown in Kansas City en route. That was good enough for me. I didn't want to get to Tahoe before I was ready, anyhow. There was plenty of time.

The flight was a bad one. The weather was fine but the pilot hit every air pocket between Miami and Kansas City. There were a lot of them. The flying didn't do anything to me other than annihilate my appetite. It had a stronger effect on a few passengers; most of them managed to hit the little paper bags that TWA thoughtfully provided, but one got the floor by mistake. It kept the trip from getting too dull.

I was very calm, considering. Again, it was that weird calm that I seem to get possessed by when I ought to be tense, by all the standard rules. The machine bit was coming on again. I had a function, a purpose. I didn't have to worry over what I might do next because I knew full well what I was going to do. I was going to wind up with Mona and the money. It was that simple.

Why on earth did I want either of them? A good question. I wasn't sure, but I was entirely sure that I did, and that was the only relevant question. So I stopped worrying about the whys.

The pilot surprised everybody with a smooth landing in K.C. I spent the twenty-five minutes between landing and takeoff in the Kansas City airport. It was a pretty new building that smelled of paint and plastic. There was a pinball machine that I took a shine to. I used to be good on pinball machines and this was an easy one. I had seven free games coming to me, and then suddenly it was time to get on the damn plane again. I found a bored little kid and told him he could play my games off for me. He stared at me in amazement and I left him there.

The rest of the ride was better. They had either changed pilots or found a brand-new atmosphere for us to fly through because the trip to Vegas was smooth as silk. I let the waitress serve me a good dinner and permitted her to refill my coffee cup two or three times. The food went down easily and stayed there. Maybe air travel was coming into its own.

I laughed, remembering the airline slogan. You know the one. *Breakfast in London, lunch in New York, dinner in Los Angeles, luggage in Buenos Aires.* That one.

It didn't work that way. My luggage and I both wound up in Las Vegas in time to watch the sun set. We got together, my luggage and I, and we took a cab to the Dunes. I'd phoned ahead for a room and it was ready for me. They don't play games in Vegas. The luxury is incredible, the price fair. The gambling brings in the money.

I took a hot shower, dried off, dressed, unpacked. I went downstairs and found the casino. The action was heavy—no town in the world has as many bored people as Vegas. Bitter little girls sitting out a divorce action, mob types looking for relaxation and not finding it, nice people like that.

Red came up six times straight on the roulette wheel,

in case you care. A man with buck teeth put a twenty-five-dollar chip down at the crap table, made seven straight passes, dragged off all but the original twenty-five, and crapped out. A stout matronly type with a silver fox stole hit the nickel jackpot on the slot machine, cashed the nickels in for half-dollars, and put every one of them back into the box.

Vegas.

I watched men win and I watched them lose. They were playing a straight house. Nothing was loaded. The house took its own little percentage and got rich. Money made in bootlegging and gunrunning and dope smuggling and whoremongering was invested quite properly in an entire town that stood as a monument to human stupidity, a boomtown in the state with the sparsest population and the densest people in the country.

Vegas.

I watched them for three hours. I had half a dozen drinks in the course of those three hours and none of them got close to me. Then I went upstairs to bed.

It was a cheap evening. I didn't risk a penny. I'm not a gambler.

12.

Las Vegas is a funny town in the morning. It's strictly a nighttime town, but one where night goes on all day long. The game rooms never close. The slots, of course, are installed next to every last cash register in the city. Breakfast was difficult. I sat at a lunch counter, drinking the first cup of coffee and smoking the first cigarette. A few feet away somebody's grandmother was making her change disappear in a chromed-up slot machine. It bothered me. Gambling before noon looks about as proper to me as laying your own sister in the front pew on Sunday morning. Call me a Puritan—that's how my mind works.

I finished the coffee and the cigarette and left the hotel. It was a short walk to the Greyhound station where a chinless clerk told me that buses left for Tahoe every two hours on the half hour. I managed to figure out without pencil or paper that one would set out at 3:30. That would be time enough.

First I had something to do.

I had to find the man. So I went looking for him, and it could have been easier and it could have been harder.

I was searching for a man I did not know. I walked around the parts of Vegas that the tourists never see—the run-down parts, the hidden parts, the parts where the neon signs are missing a letter here and there, the parts where the legal vice of gambling gives way to wilder sport.

It took three hours. For three hours I wandered and for three hours I looked very conscientiously through another pair of eyes. But after three hours I found him. Hell, he wasn't hiding. It was his business to be found. And you can always find men like him, find them in any town in the country. Waiting. Always waiting.

He was a big man. He was sitting down when I found him, sitting in a small dark café on the north side of town. His shoulders were slumped, his tie loose around his neck. He looked big anyway. He drank coffee while everybody else in the place drank beer or hard liquor. The coffee cup sat there in front of him while he ignored it and read the paper. Every once in a while when the stuff in the cup was room-temperature he would remember it was there and drain it. Seconds later a frowzy blonde would bring him a fresh one.

I picked up a bottle of beer at the bar, waved away the proffered glass and took a drink from the bottle. I carried it to his table, put it on the table and sat down opposite him.

He ignored me for a few seconds. I didn't say anything, waiting for him, and finally the newspaper went down and the eyes came up, studying me.

He said: "I don't know you."

"You don't have to."

He thought it over. He shrugged. "Talk," he said. "It's your nickel."

"I could use some nickels," I said. "A whole yardful of them."

"Yeah?"

I nodded.

"What's your scene?"

"I buy. I sell."

"Around here?"

I shook my head.

"What the hell," he said, slowly. "If this was a bust I would have heard about it by now. A yard?"

A nod from me.

"Now?"

"Fine."

He remembered his coffee and took a sip. "It's a distance," he said. "You got a short?"

I didn't. "So we'll take mine. Ride together. The dealer and the customer in the same car. It's nice when the right people run a town. No sweat. No headaches."

I followed him out of the café. Nobody looked at us on the way out. I guess they knew better. His car was parked around the corner, a new, powder-blue Olds with power everything. He drove easily and well. The Olds moved through the main section of town, along a freeway, around to the outskirts of the south side.

"Nice neighborhood," he said.

I said something appropriate. He pulled to a stop in front of a five-room ranch house with a picture window. He told me he lived there alone. We went inside and I looked at the house. It was well furnished in modern stuff that wasn't too extreme. Expensive, not flashy. I wondered whether he'd picked it himself or found an interior decorator.

"Have a seat," he said. "Relax a little."

I sat down in a chair that was far more comfortable than it looked while he disappeared. The transaction was going almost too smoothly. My man was right—it was very nice when the right people ran a town. No headaches at all.

I looked at the walls and waited for him to come back. He did, holding a little paper sack neatly rolled. "Thirty nickels for a dollar," he said. "Bargain day at the zoo. You picked a good time. The store is overstocked so we have a sale. You want to count 'em?"

I shook my head. If he wanted to cheat me, a count wouldn't make any difference. I was reaching for my wallet when I remembered something else that I needed.

"A kit," I said. "I could use a kit."

He looked amused. "For you?"

"For anybody."

He shrugged. "That's a dime more."

I told him that was okay. He went away again and came back with a flat leather box that looked as though it ought to contain a set of draftsman's tools. I took the box and the sack and gave him one hundred and ten dollars—

a dollar and a dime in his language. He folded them twice and stuck them into his shirt pocket. For small change, maybe.

On the way back to the center of town he became almost talkative. He asked me what I was doing in Vegas and I told him I was just passing through, which was true enough.

"I travel a lot," I said. "Wherever there are people. Places get warm if you stay too long."

"Depends how well connected you are."

I shrugged.

"See me when you hit Vegas next," he said. "I'm always in the same place. Or ask and they'll take a message for me. Sometimes the price gets better than it was today. We can always deal."

"Sure."

Just before he let me out of the car he started to laugh. I asked him what was so funny.

"Nothing," he said. "I was just thinking. It's such a groovy business. Depressions don't even touch us. Isn't that a gas?"

I left my bags in my room at the Dunes. I wasn't ready to check out, not for the time being. And at 3:30 I caught the bus to Tahoe. It was not crowded. Neither were the roads and we made good time. It was a good trip—hot sun, clear air. I sat by myself and looked out the window and smoked cigarettes. The bus was air-conditioned and the smoke from the end of my cigarette trailed up along the window pane and disappeared.

We hit Lake Tahoe in time for dinner. And I was hungry. I found the washroom in the bus station first, tossed a quarter in a slot and let myself into a private cubicle with fresh towels and a big wash basin. I washed up, straightened my tie and felt almost human.

I ate a big dinner in a hurry. But I barely tasted the food. Then I left the restaurant and made the rounds.

It was too early at first but I was looking anyway. If she was in Tahoe she would be gambling. And there just weren't that many casinos. Sooner or later we were going to run into each other.

In the first casino I went over to the crap table and made dollar bets against the shooter. When my turn came up I passed the dice and left. I was a few dollars ahead and could not have cared less.

In the second casino I put the crap table profits into a slot machine. I kept looking around for her but didn't find her. So I left.

Then I passed a men's shop, saw a hat in the window, and remembered that it might be better all across the board if I saw her before she saw me. A hat was supposed to be a good prop, altering the shape of your head or something. There are places where a man with a hat on stands out. The owners themselves don't know enough to take their hats off inside.

I went inside and bought the hat. It was an Italian import, a Borsalino, and it was priced at twenty bucks. It seemed sort of silly, shelling out twenty bucks for a hat I was going to wear once and throw away. But I reminded myself that it no longer mattered what anything cost. A

five-dollar hat might do as well, but I was not in a store
that sold five-dollar hats. I bought the Borsalino and
wore it out of the store.

It didn't look bad. It had a high crown and a narrow
brim. It was black, very soft.

I studied my reflection in the store window. I experi-
mented until the hat looked good and did its job well.
Then I went to the next casino.

I picked them up a few minutes past nine in the Charlton
Room. I was nursing a bourbon sour and watching the
roulette wheel when I saw them. They were at the crap
table just a few yards away. I took my drink with me and
moved off.

I had known he would be with her. I could even have
told you what he looked like. Black hair—black, not dark
brown—and broad shoulders and expensive clothes. Hair
combed too neatly, hairs always perfectly in place.
Clothes worn too well, too casual to be true. And an easy
laugh. The looks and effect of two types only, gigolos and
fags. He wasn't a fag.

I knew the rules of the game. She would give him a
certain amount of money to play with and he would keep
it, win or lose. Of course he would tell her that he'd lost,
and she could believe it or not, depending upon her own
state of mind.

What she probably didn't know was that he also got a
cut of her net losses. This was the house's idea, so that he
would keep her playing as long as possible. She couldn't
have known this, but she wouldn't have cared anyway.

The money didn't matter to her, not if she was getting all that she was paying for.

I tried to hate the gigolo and couldn't. He wasn't hurting me, for one thing. For another, the reason I knew so much about his particular method of earning a living was that I had played the same record myself from time to time. It's tough feeling superior to yourself.

She had the dice now. But she wasn't conforming to the stereotype of the woman with the kept man in her pocket. Usually a woman in that position is trying her damnedest to have all the fun in the world. A perpetual smile, wild gesturing and brittle laughter. And underneath it all a profound uneasiness. The last shows up in the hand clutching too tightly at an elbow, the laugh at something not at all funny, the general impression of being a semi-competent actress at a very important audition. Auditioning for what? The world? Or for herself?

But Mona wasn't like that. She seemed so desperately bored it was astounding. The guy next to her was pretty as a picture and she hardly seemed to know he was there. The action at the crap table was as fast as it ever gets and it bored her stiff. She threw the dice, not as if she hated them, but as if she was trying to get rid of them.

I couldn't keep my eyes off her. I kept looking at her face and trying to reconcile the beauty and, yes, innocence, with the person I knew she was. I looked at her, stared at her, and once again took all the pieces of the puzzle and glued them together with library paste. I tried to imagine living with her, and then I tried to imagine living without her, and I realized that either alternative was equally impossible.

Looking at Mona made me remember the other girl, the girl at the Eden Roc. I had forgotten her name, but I remembered that she lived in the Bronx and worked for an insurance company and wanted to have fun on her vacation. I remembered the love we had made, and I remembered how she looked when she dropped off to sleep. I remembered thinking how good it would be to fall in love with her, and marry her, and live with her.

But I had forgotten more than her name. I tried to picture her face and failed. I tried to recall her voice and missed. The only picture I got was an abstract one composed of the qualities of the girl herself. They were fine qualities. Mona lacked almost all of them but beauty.

Yet everything about Mona stayed in my mind.

I found a slot machine that took nickels and gave it one of mine. I pulled the lever very slowly and watched the dials to see what would happen. I got a bell, a cherry and a lemon. The nickel slots, I discovered, were more fun than the dollar slots. I couldn't win anything and I couldn't lose anything. I could only waste time and watch the dials spin.

I tried again. This time I lucked out with three of something or other. Twelve nickels galloped back at me.

I could not live with her and I could not live without her. An interesting problem. I had imagined, earlier, what it would be like to have Mona for a wife. I knew how her mind worked. Keith was dead, not because she had hated him, not because she had wanted me, but because she no longer needed him. He was excess baggage. And, because he was excess baggage, he had been jettisoned in flight. It would make no tremendous difference if I took his place. Not that she would kill me, but that she would leave me, or do her damnedest to make me leave her. It would not be any good at all.

And I knew damn well what would happen if I tried living without her. Every night, no matter where I was or who I was with, I would think about her. Every night I would picture her face, and remember her body, and wonder where she was and who she was sleeping with and what she was wearing and—

One of the most common murder patterns in the world is that of a man who murders a woman, proclaiming *If I can't have her, nobody can.* It had never made any sense to me whatsoever. Now I was beginning to understand.

But I had decided that I could not kill her.

I could not live with her or without her. I could not kill her. And I certainly did not intend to kill myself. It looked insoluble.

I dropped another nickel in the slot machine and thought that I was very clever to have hit the answer all by myself. I pulled the lever and watched the dials.

They hit one more casino after that one. It was midnight when they left the second one, midnight or a little after. They'd had a few drinks and they both seemed a little bit high. They walked and I followed them to the Roycroft. It was the best hotel in Tahoe and I had more or less figured all along that they'd be staying there.

I waited outside, then hit the lobby after they were already in the elevator. I looked around the lobby but this time I didn't even notice the money-smell in the air. Hell, the Eden Roc was just as plush. And I'd paid the tab there all by myself. Well, almost. At any rate, I was getting tougher to impress.

I saw the bell captain and walked over to him. He looked me over carefully from the new Borsalino to Keith's shoes on my feet. Then his eyes and mine got together.

"That couple that just came in," I said. "Did you notice them?"

"I may have."

Straight from Hollywood, this one. I smiled gently. "Mighty fine-looking couple," I said. "You know, I bet you aren't too observant. Here they are, staying here, and you don't notice them at all."

He didn't say anything.

"What I mean," I said, "is that I'll bet you twenty dollars you don't even know what room they're staying in."

He thought about it. "Awright," he said. "Eight-oh-four."

I gave him the twenty. "That was very good," I said. "But it doesn't move me. I'll bet you a hundred you don't have a key that would open their door."

He almost smiled. "No trouble," he said.

"Not for the world."

He vanished. He returned. He traded me a key for a hundred-dollar bill.

"If there's trouble," he said, "you don't know where you got that key."

"I found it under a flat stone."

"You got it," he said. "Keep it quiet, huh?"

"Sure."

He looked me over, very carefully. "I don't think I get it," he said.

"For a hundred and twenty you don't have to."

He shrugged elaborately. "Curiosity," he said. "The human comedy."

"It killed the cat."

Another profound shrug. "You her husband?"

I shook my head.

"I didn't think so. But—"

"That guy upstairs with her," I said. "You've seen him? The one with the shoulders and the hair?"

The expression on his face told me just how much regard he had for the boy upstairs.

"*He's* her husband," I explained. "I'm her jealous lover. The bitch is two-timing me."

He sighed. It was better than a shrug. "You don't want to talk straight," he said, "maybe I'll watch television. They're funnier on television."

He had a right to his opinion. I found a chair in the lobby and sat in it, giving them time to get started at whatever they were going to do. The ceiling was sound-proofed and I tried to count the little holes in it. I'm not enough of an idiot to count the holes themselves, of course. I count the holes in one of the squares, and then I see how many squares there are on the whole ceiling. And then I multiply it out.

What the hell. It's something to do.

I finished a cigarette, then got up and put another one in my mouth. I set it on fire and dragged hard on it. I took the smoke way down deep in my lungs and held onto it. Then I let it out, slowly, in a single thin column that held together for a long while. You can get slightly dizzy that way, but the dizziness can make you feel more confident. I felt very confident.

I walked over to the elevator. The op was reading the morning paper. He was studying the morning line. It is a hell of a thing when you live in Nevada and still have to play the horses. I shook my head sadly and he looked up at me.

"Eight," I said.

He didn't say anything. He piloted the car to the eighth floor and I got out. The door closed and he sailed down to the main floor again to study the racing form. I hoped he would lose every race. I felt very mean.

I walked one way, came to a room number, and found out that I was headed the wrong way. I turned around and worked my way to 804. There was a *Do Not Disturb* sign on it which somehow seemed very funny. I thought that it would be fun to knock so that they could tell me to go away.

I didn't.

Instead I finished the cigarette. I walked all the way back to the elevator to dunk it in an urn filled with sand instead of grinding it into the thick carpet. Then I walked all the way back and stood in front of the door some more.

A sliver of light came through the door at the bottom.

Not much. As if one little lamp were turned on.

Which meant the stage was set.

I took the key out of my pocket. I stuck it into the lock. It went in soundlessly and turned soundlessly. I said a silent prayer of thanks to the mercenary bell captain. A penknife is effective, but it is not subtle. I felt very much like being subtle.

It was a very nice hotel. The door did not even squeak. I opened it all the way and there they were.

The main light was off but they had left the closet light on, which was very coy of them. It let me see without squinting. There was quite a bit to see.

She was on the bed. Her head was back on the pillow and her eyes were closed. Her legs were bent and parted.

He was between them. He was earning his keep and working very hard at it. He seemed to be enjoying it. So did she. But there was no way of telling with either of them.

I stepped inside, very thankful that Keith's shoes didn't squeak. I turned and closed the door. They did not hear me or notice me in any way.

They were too busy.

For several very long seconds I watched them. Once, long ago, when I had been too young to know what it was all about, I happened to watch my mother and father making love. I didn't really know what they were doing. But I knew what Mona and her friend were doing and there was something almost hypnotic about the performance. Maybe it was the rhythm. I'm not sure.

Then it was time. I really wanted to come on with

something extremely clever but my brain refused to supply anything really appropriate. It was a shame. You don't get too many opportunities like that one.

But nothing clever came to mind. And I didn't have all night. So what I said, finally, was about as trite as you can get. Concise and to the point, but not very original.

I said: "Hello, Mona."

13.

They didn't even finish what they were doing. They stopped at once. He rolled away from her and came up on the balls of his feet while she lay there trying to cover herself with her hands. A silly gesture.

He could have dressed, tied his shoes, and walked right past me. I had no quarrel with him. I wasn't ready to run around proclaiming my undying love for him, but I wasn't ready to kick his face in, either. He was out of his element. A bedroom bouncing-bee had turned into more than that and it was time for him to pick up his pants and go home.

That wasn't his style. He could read it only one way—I had intruded on his privacy, interrupted his sport, made him look foolish. That was the only diagnosis those beautiful blue eyes could report to that muscle-bound brain, and there was only one way that body could react to that sort of information.

He rushed me.

He must have played football once. He came with his head way down and his arms outstretched. Anybody looks silly enough like that but he looked sillier. He was nude, and *all* men look ridiculous nude. But there was something else. He rushed me, and I stared at the top of his head, and I saw that every last strand of hair remained magically in place.

I kicked him in the face.

He did a little back-flip and wound up sitting on his can. The point of the shoe had come into pleasant contact with his jaw and he was dizzy—unhurt, unmarked, but dizzy.

He tried to get up.

The funny thing is that I still wasn't mad at him at all. But I knew that I had to show him just where he stood in the overall scheme of things. I did not want him in my hair. I had more important things on my mind than the stupid son-of-a-bitch.

I did not bother playing fair. That would have been stupid. I waited until he got halfway up and then I kicked his face in again. It was a better kick this time. It split his lip and took out a tooth. He wouldn't be pretty for the next month or so.

He wouldn't be able to earn a living, either. Because I put the next kick between his legs. He made a little-girl sound way in the back of his throat that turned into a strangled moan before he was done with it.

Then he blacked out.

I turned to Mona. She was all wrapped up in a robe now. I could tell that she was frightened but she managed to hide most of the fear. I had to give her credit.

I waited her out. Finally she tried a smile, gave it up, and sighed. "I'm supposed to say something," she said. "I suppose. But where do I start?"

I lighted a cigarette.

"I would have come to Miami," she said. "Except I was afraid if we made contact too quickly—"

"Shut up."

She looked as though she had been slapped.

"You don't have to talk," I said. "I'll talk. But first we get rid of your friend."

"He wasn't my friend."

"You looked pretty friendly there for a few seconds."

She swallowed. "He wasn't like you, Joe. Nobody was. You were always the best. You—"

"Save it," I said. I was annoyed at her for trying that. She should have been able to do better. "We're getting rid of your friend," I said again. "Then we talk."

I walked over to the phone, picked it up and asked for the bell captain. He was there in no time.

"Upstairs," I said, "in eight-oh-four. A little job I'd like you to do for me. A favor."

"This is the jealous lover?"

"The same."

"Still feeling generous?"

"Very. Still greedy?"

A low chuckle. "Be right up," he said, and rang off.

I checked Hair-and-Shoulders. He was still out. "Dress him," I told her. "In a hurry. Get his clothes on. You don't have to make him look beautiful but get him dressed."

She went to work.

"The bell captain'll be here in a minute," I went on. "Don't get cute. You won't be able to carry it off. I'll take us both to the chair if I have to."

"You wouldn't."

"You sure of that?"

No answer. She went on dressing him and I waited for the bell captain. A few minutes later there was a knock on the door, quite discreet, and I let him in.

I gave him another hundred. "Our friend had an accident," I said. "Too much to drink. Then he fell down and hurt himself. Somebody ought to take him home."

He looked at Shoulders, then at me. "A lovely accident," he said. "It couldn't happen to a more deserving fellow. Not stiff, is he?"

I shook my head. "But tired," I said. "I'm tired, too. I'd carry him back to his apartment but I really need my sleep. I thought maybe you'd take care of him for me."

He smiled.

"One more thing," I said. "The lady and I would like a certain amount of privacy. For quite awhile. No phone calls, no knocks at the door. Can you take care of that?"

He looked at Mona, then back at me. "A cinch."

I waited there while he picked up Shoulders. He draped him over his own shoulder and smiled sadly at me. Then he carried him out of the room like a sack of wet laundry and I closed the door after him and slid the bolt home.

She turned to look at me. This time her eyes were very wide with the fear showing through them. Breathing wasn't easy for her.

"Are you going to kill me, Joe?"

I shook my head.

"Then what do you want? Money? You can have half of it, Joe. There's so much. More than I need, more than you need. You can have half. Is that fair enough? I'll give you half, I was going to give you half anyway, and—"

"Don't lie to me."

"It's the truth, Joe. I—"

"Don't lie."

She stopped talking and looked at me. Her eyes were hurt. She was telling me with her eyes that I shouldn't call her a liar, it wasn't nice. I should be nice to a pretty girl like her.

"No lies," I said. "We're going to play a brand new game. It's called *To Tell the Truth*. Like on television."

She looked very nervous. I lighted a cigarette and handed it to her. She needed it.

"You were damned good," I told her. "You were so good that you didn't even have to cover all the loopholes. You let me see the holes in your story and I wrote them off as coincidences. That was very good."

I remembered the Hitchcock movie I saw in Cleveland. You can get away with coincidences if your direction is tight enough. And Mona was a fine director.

"Let's start at the beginning," I said. "Keith was supposed to be a heroin importer. That was his business. And you weren't supposed to know a thing about it. That should have sounded fishy right at the beginning. How in the hell would he run a game like that without you knowing? And why would he take you along to Atlantic City while he was working a deal? He wasn't on vacation—he was hauling a load for Max Treger and you knew the score right from the start. That was a cute bit."

She looked unhappy.

"Here's the way I figure it," I went on. "You were at the station. You saw me pick up Keith's bags. He didn't, but you did. You could have stopped me right then and there but that was too easy. Your mind was starting to buzz, wheels were turning. There might be an angle in it for you. So you didn't say a word.

"So I picked up the luggage, and then you picked me up. You took your time, maybe, but you sure as hell didn't sit on your hands. You found me on the beach, made a date with me, and met me on the beach that night. And you let me figure out who you were by inches. L. Keith Brassard's pretty little wife. You let me take two and two and put them together until they came up five."

"I liked you."

"You were nuts about me. You were right on hand the next morning with the chambermaid routine. You knew I had the heroin but that was all you knew. Somewhere there had to be something for you. You were sniffing around. Hell, even the way you woke me up was beautiful. You shook me and blabbered about finding Keith's bags in my closet. It was lovely. You didn't even have to fake being confused. You were confused, all right. You couldn't find the horse and that confused the daylights out of you."

I stopped and shook my head. Saying it aloud was

somehow different from running it through my mind. Everything fit perfectly into place and there was no room left for doubt. It all added up with nothing out of place.

"If the horse had been there you probably would have disappeared with it. God knows what you would have done with it—maybe tried to swing a deal on your own, maybe tried to sell it back to Keith or something. God knows. But you saw that you couldn't get it back. And your mind went on working. Maybe you could use me, get me to kill Keith for you. That was a good idea, wasn't it?

"And you played it perfectly, made me suggest it, let me act as though it was my idea from the beginning. You were tired of him. He was beginning to get in the way and you wanted out. But you wanted the money and maybe I could get it for you. You were cool about it, Mona. You were perfect."

"It wasn't like that, Joe—"

"The hell it wasn't. It was that simple. So simple it never occurred to me. You faked everything beautifully. Even the bed part. You pretended to fall in love with me. You acted so perfectly I fell on my face."

Her face was funny. Very sad, mournful. I looked into her eyes and tried to probe. They were opaque.

So I let go of it. I sat there and looked at her and she looked back at me. I smoked another cigarette. When she talked, finally, her voice was just a little bit more than a whisper. There was no pretense left. I knew that she would tell me the truth now because there was no longer any reason for her to lie. I knew, I understood. And, as a result, I could no longer be lied to. The lies would only bounce at her.

She said: "There's more, Joe."

"There is?"

A slow nod.

"Then tell me about it. I'm a good listener."

"You'd like to believe it was just the money," she said. "It wasn't. Oh, in the beginning the money was most of it. I'll admit that. But then . . . then we were together and it was . . . more . . . than just the money. It was us, too. I thought about what it would be like, you and me together, and I thought about it and—"

She broke off. The room was noisy with silence. I drew on my cigarette.

"And somewhere along the line it turned into just the money again. Because you didn't need me any more."

"Maybe."

"What else?"

She thought it over for a moment or two before answering. "Because you killed him," she said.

"Huh?"

"You killed him," she repeated. "Oh, we were both guilty. Legally, that is. I know all that. But . . . inside, when I thought about it, you were the one who killed him. And if I went to you I killed him, too. But if I was alone by myself it didn't work out that way. I could pretend he just . . . died. That somebody killed him but that I myself had nothing to do with it."

"Did it work?"

She sighed. "Maybe. I don't know. It was starting to

work. Then I thought about you and I knew you were waiting for me in Miami and wondering what was wrong. And I thought that you had to get something for . . . what you did. That's when I sent you the money. The three thousand dollars."

"I didn't know you had a conscience."

She managed a smile. "I'm not that bad."

"No?"

"Not that bad. Bad, but not rotten. Not really."

She was right. And I realized, somehow, that I had known this all along. A strange sensation.

"What now, Joe?"

Her words shattered silence. I knew what was coming next but it didn't seem right to tell her. I wanted to stretch the moment out for half of eternity. I didn't want *what now* to come up just yet. Neither of us was ready for it.

"Joe?"

I didn't answer.

"You said you weren't going to kill me. Did you change your mind, Joe?"

I told her I wasn't going to kill her.

"Then what do you want?"

I put out my cigarette. I took a breath. The air in the room was very thick, or seemed to be. Breathing was difficult.

"To marry me?"

I nodded.

"You want to marry me," she said. Her voice had a light, almost airy quality to it. She was talking as much to herself as to me, testing the words. "Well, all right. I . . .

it's not very romantic. But if that's what you want, it's all right with me. I won't argue."

I heard her words and listened past them. I tried once more for a picture of marital bliss and once more it wouldn't come into focus. The only image I got was the one I'd visualized earlier. It wouldn't work the way she wanted it.

I wished to heaven it would. But it wouldn't, not without my little solution. My method was the only way, much as I was beginning to dislike it.

So I sat next to her, close to her, and I smiled gently at her. She returned the smile, hesitantly. Her world was beginning to return to focus now. There we were, smiling at each other, and pretty soon everything was going to be all right. A slight change in plans, of course, but nothing drastic.

I said: "I'm sorry, Mona."

Then I hit her. I got the right spot, just over the bridge of the nose, and I did not hit too hard. A hard blow there breaks off parts of the frontal bone and sends it into the brain. But I was gentle. All I did was knock her out—she lost consciousness at once and fell very limp into my arms.

When she came to a few minutes later there was a gag in her mouth. Strips of bedsheet tied her feet together and other strips held her hands behind her back.

She stared at me and the expression on her face was one of sheer and unadulterated terror.

"Someday you'll adjust to this," I told her. "Someday you'll understand. I don't expect you to understand now.

But you will, in time."

I took the two packages from my jacket pocket. The paper sack, tightly rolled, and the neat leather kit. I unrolled the paper sack and took out one of the little black capsules. I opened the leather kit and let her see what was inside.

She gasped.

"Funny," I said. "The way we always come back to this. Keith sold it, I bought it. You know the funniest part of it? I had to pay good money for this stuff. I threw away a boxful of it to frame Keith, left a fortune's worth to make things look groovy for the New York cops. And here we are again. Full circle."

I took the small spoon from the leather kit. It was the kind of spoon you stir your coffee with in a café espresso in Greenwich Village. I settled the capsule on the spoon, then got out my cigarette lighter and flicked it. I held the spoon over the flame and watched the heroin melt. My hand was surprisingly steady.

I looked at Mona. Her eyes on the flame from the lighter were the eyes of a cat in front of a fire. Hot ice.

"You're just too independent," I said. "You live inside yourself. And when people take too much from you, too much *of* you, you run away and hide. That's no good."

She didn't answer, of course. Hell, there was a gag in her mouth. But I wondered what she was thinking.

"So you're going to be a little less independent. You're going to have something to depend on."

I picked up the hypodermic needle. I pushed the plunger all the way in, stuck the tip of the needle into the melted heroin on the spoon. When I let the plunger out again the needle filled with liquid heroin.

The needle looked very large. Very dangerous. Mona's eyes were round and I could hear the wheels turning in her head. She didn't want to believe it but she had to.

"Don't be frightened," I said, stupidly. "It isn't that bad, not when you have money. You take so many shots a day and you function almost as well as a normal person. You know what group has the largest percentage of addicts in the country? Doctors. Because they have access to the stuff. They're morphine addicts, generally, but it's about the same thing. And they get all they need. If you never have withdrawal symptoms it's not so bad. Not as rough on your system as alcohol, for example."

She didn't even hear me. And I was being cruel, taking too much time to do what I had to do. I stopped talking.

I found a good spot in the fleshy part of her thigh. Later I could graduate her to the main line, the big vein that led straight to the heart. But skin-popping was fine for the time being. I didn't want to get her sick from an overdose.

I held up the needle. I stuck it into her and rammed the plunger all the way in. She tried to scream when it hit but the gag was in her way and the only sound that came out was a small snort through her nose.

Then the heroin hit and she went off to Dreamland.

14.

It took her an hour to come out of it. She was still slightly drugged so I took the gag off. There wasn't much chance of her giving out with a yell. I asked her how she felt.

"All right," she said. "I suppose."

We talked for a few minutes about very little. I put the gag back on and went downstairs. There was a newstand in the lobby and I picked up a few paperback books. I went back to the room and sat around reading until it was time for her next shot.

She didn't fight the second quite as much as the first.

That set the pattern. We stayed there for three days, with me going down intermittently for food. Every four or five hours she got her shot. The rest of the time we stayed in the room. Once or twice I untied her completely and we made love, but it was not very good at all. It would get better.

"I'm sick of Tahoe," I told her one morning. "I want a few grand. I'll buy a car and we'll go to Vegas."

"Use your own money."

"I haven't got enough."

"Then go to hell."

I could have hit her, or threatened her, or merely ordered her to give me the money. But this was as good a time as any for the test. Instead I shrugged and waited.

I waited until her shot was half an hour overdue. Then she called my name.

"What's the matter?"

"I . . . want a shot."

"That's nice. I want four grand. Where are you keeping it?"

She shrugged as if it didn't matter. But I could see the need beginning to build in her, the nervousness behind those eyes, the tension buried in those muscles. She told me where the money was. I found it, then got out the kit and cooked her up another fix. This time she was visibly grateful when the heroin took hold. It was a mainline shot this time and it reached her faster than the others.

I paid cash for the car, a nice new Buick with a lot under the hood and so much chrome outside that it looked like a twenty-fifth-century cathouse on wheels. I loaded her into the car and we drove back to Vegas. She was very docile on the trip. We got to Vegas, reclaimed my room at the Dunes, and it was time for her shot.

I do not know how long it takes to turn a person into an addict. I do not know how long it took with Mona. Addiction is a gradual process. I merely pushed the process along, let the addiction pile up. She became a little more nearly hooked with every passing shot. Hooked physically and emotionally. It's a double-barreled thing.

✿

"I'm leaving," she said.

I looked at her. It was two in the afternoon, a Friday afternoon. We were still at the Dunes. Two hours ago she had had a shot. In two hours she'd be due for another.

She was wearing a red jersey dress with a simple string of pearls around her neck. Her shoes were black suede with high heels. And she was telling me that she was leaving.

I asked her what she meant.

"Leaving," she said. "Leaving you. Walking out, Joe. You don't tie me up any more. It's very sweet of you. So I'm walking out on you."

"And not coming back?"

"And not coming back."

"You're hooked," I told her. "You're a junkie. Try walking out and you'll wind up crawling back. Who do you think you're kidding?"

"I'm not hooked."

"You really believe that?"

"I know it."

"Then I know who you're kidding," I said. "You're kidding yourself. So long."

She left. And I waited for her to come back, waited past the time when the shot was due.

And she came back.

She did not look like the same girl. Her face was a dead fishbelly white and her hands couldn't stay still. She was twitching uncontrollably. She hurried into the room and threw herself into a chair.

"You walked out," I said. "Don't tell me you're back already. That's a pretty quick trip."

"Please," she said. Just that—*please*.

"Something wrong?"

"I need it," she said. "I need it, damn you. You're right, I was wrong. Now give me a shot."

I laughed at her. Not out of cruelty, not because I was pleased. I laughed at her so that she would get the full picture. She had to know, inside and out, that she was hooked. The sooner she knew it, the more deeply the addiction would run.

I watched her twitch with pain and sheer need. I listened to her beg for the shot and I pretended not to hear her. I watched her scramble around on her hands and knees looking for the hypo. I'd hidden it. She couldn't find it.

Then she stood up and tore that fine red dress all the way down. She removed her bra, her underclothing. She cupped her breasts in her hands and offered them to me.

"Anything," she said. "Anything—"

I brought out the needle and fixed her. I watched the pain drain from her features and I stroked her body until she stopped shivering. Then I held her very gently in my arms while she cried.

After that it was all downhill. I didn't even have to threaten her in order to get her to agree. Whatever I said, went. It was that simple.

A justice of the peace married us in Vegas. He asked us the time-honored questions. I said I did and she said she did, and he pronounced us man and wife. We moved out of the Dunes and into three rooms and a kitchen on the North side of town. She transferred her money to a Vegas bank and opened an account with a Vegas broker.

And I built up a close relationship with the big man who hangs out in the café and drinks cold coffee. Every five days he sells me one hundred dollars' worth of capsules. Every four hours Mona takes a shot. Six capsules a day. A thirty-pound monkey, in junkie argot. A twenty-pound monkey for us, because I get wholesale prices. The quantity buyer always has the edge, even when the commodity is an illegal one.

As if it made a difference. As if ten dollars a day or twenty or thirty or forty dollars a day could have the slightest effect on us. My wife has an alarming amount of money. And it looks as though it's going to last forever, too, because the broker took good care of us. He put part of the dough in bonds, part in common stocks, the rest in high-yield real estate. We can live big on income and never look at the principal. There is a point where you stop counting money; it is wealth then, not just money. Ten dollars, twenty dollars, thirty dollars—it couldn't matter less.

The habit doesn't bite. Mona is not one of the junkies I see from time to time in the café, hollow-eyed and shivering, haggling with the big man. For a drug addict, Mona is sitting pretty.

But there are times when I look at her, at this very beautiful and very wealthy woman who happens to be my wife and who also happens to be an addict. I look at her and I remember the woman she used to be, the free and independent one. I remember the first night on the beach, and I remember other nights and other places, and I know that something is gone forever. She is not so much alive now. The face is the same and the body is the same but something has changed. The eyes, maybe. Or the deep darkness behind them.

The bird in your cage is not the same bird as the wild thing you caught in the forest. There is a difference.

So many things could happen. Some fine day the big man could disappear forever from the café. She'd be a deep-sea diver with her air-hose cut, and we'd burrow through Vegas turning over flat stones to find a connection, and I would have the rare privilege of watching Mona die inside. By inches.

Or a raid, and cold turkey behind bars, banging her head against the walls and screaming sandpaper curses at the guards. Or an overdose because some idiot somewhere in the long powdery chain forgot to cut the heroin when it was his turn. An overdose, with her veins blue and her eyes bulging and death there before she gets the needle out of her arm.

So many things—

I think she's happy now. Once she got used to being addicted—how do you get used to addiction? A good question—once she got used to it, she began to enjoy it. Strange but true. When you have an itch you enjoy scratching it. Now she looks forward to her shots, takes pleasure in them. A certain amount of reality is lost, of course. But she seems to think that what she gets in its place more than compensates for reality. She may be right. The real world is often vastly overrated.

Strange.

"You should try it," she'll say now and then. "I wish I could tell you what it's like. It's really something. Like a bomb going off, you dig?"

She retreats into hip talk when she gets high.

"You should make it, Joe. Just one little joy-bomb to get you moving. So you can see what it's like."

A strange life in a strange world.

A funny thing happened yesterday.

I was giving her her four P.M. fix. I cooked the heroin, sucked it up in the hypo, picked up her leg and hunted around for the vein. She was just at the point where she needed the shot and in another five or ten minutes she would have started to shake. I found the vein and fixed her and watched the graceful smile spread on her face before she went under.

Then I was washing the spoon, getting ready to put the kit away. Some junkies don't take good care of their equipment. They die of infection that way. I'm always careful.

I was washing the spoon, as I said, and then I was putting it away. I stopped—maybe I should say I slowed down—and then I was picking up another little capsule filled with funny white powder, putting it on the spoon.

I wanted to take a shot myself.

Silly. Her words hadn't done it, her invitations to find out what it was all about. I wasn't a kid looking for kicks.

So naturally I put the cap away. And I put the spoon away and put the syringe away. I locked up the kit and the bag of capsules. Even in Vegas you never know when some cop is going to decide his arrest quota is off for the month. I never leave things lying around.

I put everything away.

For the time being.

And I've been thinking about it ever since. I have a damned good idea what is going to happen. It may be the next time I give her a shot, or a week from then, or a month. She'll slip away from me, with the same grateful smile fading slowly on the same sad and lovely face, and I will begin to wash the works.

Then I'll take a shot of my own.

Not for kicks or thrills or joy. Not for pleasure or escape, not as a reward and not as penance. Not because I crave the life of a junkie. I don't.

Something else. To share with her, maybe. Or maybe the nagging knowledge that every time the heroin takes hold of her she slips that much further away from me. Something like that, I don't know. But one of these days or weeks or months I'll take that shot for myself.

I think we're going to be very something together. Whatever it is, at least it will be together. And that's what I wanted, isn't it?

THE END